"I want a partner, not a possessor,"

Mari said shakily. "I thought I knew something about men until just now. But I don't know anything at all. And I'll be delighted to go back home and join a convent!"

"After one kiss? Was it that bad?" he taunted.

"You scare me, big man," she said, backing away from him. "I'll stick to men my own age from now on, thanks. I'm afraid you know more about making love than I'll ever learn."

Ward smiled slowly, surprised by her frankness. "I probably do. But you're sweet, all the same."

"Years too young for a man like you," she said, still trying to catch her breath.

He folded his arms thoughtfully. "But I could be tempted..."

Dear Reader,

Welcome to Silhouette. Experience the magic of the wonderful world where two people fall in love. Meet heroines who will make you cheer for their happiness, and heroes (be they the boy next door or a handsome, mysterious stranger) who will win your heart. Silhouette Romances reflect the magic of love—sweeping you away with books that will make you laugh and cry, heartwarming, poignant stories that will move you time and time again.

In the next few months, we're publishing romances by many of your all-time favorites, such as Diana Palmer, Brittany Young, Emilie Richards and Arlene James. Your response to these authors and other authors of Silhouette Romances has served as a touchstone for us, and we're pleased to bring you more books with Silhouette's distinctive medley of charm, wit and—above all—*romance*.

I hope you enjoy this book and the many stories to come. Experience the magic!

Sincerely,

Tara Hughes
Senior Editor
Silhouette Books

DIANA PALMER
Unlikely Lover

Silhouette Romance

Published by Silhouette Books New York

America's Publisher of Contemporary Romance

SILHOUETTE BOOKS
300 E. 42nd St., New York, N.Y. 10017

ISBN: 0-373-08472-2

First Silhouette Books printing December 1986

Books by Diana Palmer

Silhouette Romance

Darling Enemy #254
Roomful of Roses #301
Heart of Ice #314
Passion Flower #328
Soldier of Fortune #340
After the Music #406
Champagne Girl #436
Unlikely Lover #472

Silhouette Special Edition

Heather's Song #33
The Australian #239

Silhouette Desire

The Cowboy and the Lady #12
September Morning #26
Friends and Lovers #50
Fire and Ice #80
Snow Kisses #102
Diamond Girl #110
The Rawhide Man #157
Lady Love #175
Cattleman's Choice #193
The Tender Stranger #230
Love by Proxy #252
Eye of the Tiger #271
Loveplay #289
Rawhide and Lace #306

DIANA PALMER

is a prolific romance writer who got her start as a newspaper reporter. Accustomed to the daily deadlines of a journalist, she has no problem with writer's block. In fact, she averages a book every two months. Mother of a young son, Diana met and married her husband within one week: "It was just like something from one of my books."

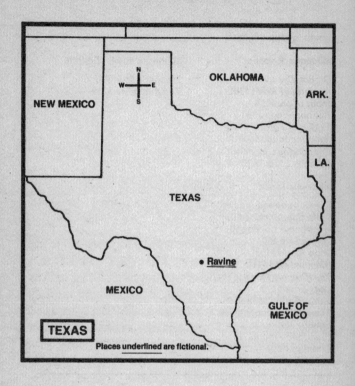

OKLAHOMA

NEW MEXICO

ARK.

LA.

TEXAS

• Ravine

MEXICO

GULF OF MEXICO

TEXAS

Places underlined are fictional.

Chapter One

Ward Jessup went to the supper table rubbing his big hands together, his green eyes like dark emeralds in a face like a Roman's, perfectly sculpted under hair as thick and black as crow feathers. He was enormously tall, big and rangy looking, with an inborn elegance and grace that came from his British ancestors. But Ward himself was all-American. All Oklahoman, with a trace of Cherokee and a sprinkling of Irish that gave him his taciturn stubbornness and his cutting temper, respectively.

"You look mighty proud of yourself," Lillian huffed, bringing in platters of beef and potatoes and yeast rolls.

"Why shouldn't I?" he asked. "Things are going pretty well. Grandmother's leaving, did she tell you? She's going to stay with my sister. Lucky, lucky Belinda!"

Lillian lifted her eyes to the ceiling. "I must have pleased you, Lord, for all my prayers to be so suddenly answered," she said.

Ward chuckled as he reached for the platter of sliced roast beef. "I thought you two were great buddies."

"And we stay that way as long as I run fast, keep my mouth shut and pretend that I like cooking five meals at a time."

"She may come back."

"I'll quit," was the gruff reply. "She's only been here four months, and I'm ready to apply for that cookhouse job over at Wade's."

"You'd wind up in the house with Conchita, helping to look after the twins," he returned.

She grinned, just for an instant. Could have been a muscle spasm, he thought.

"I like kids." Lillian glared at him, brushing back wiry strands of gray hair that seemed to match her hatchet nose, long chin and beady little black eyes. "Why don't you get married and have some?" she added.

His thick eyebrows raised a little. They were perfect like his nose, even his mouth. He was handsome. He could have had a dozen women by crooking his finger, but he dated only occasionally, and he never brought women home. He never got serious, either. He hadn't since that Caroline person had almost led him to the altar, only to turn around at the last minute and marry his cousin Bud, thinking that, because Bud's last name was Jessup, he'd do as well as Ward. Besides, Bud was much easier to manage. The marriage had only lasted a few weeks, however, just until Bud had discovered that Caroline's main interest was in how much of his small inheritance she could spend on herself. He had divorced her, and she had come rushing back to Ward, all in tears. But somewhere along the way Ward had opened his eyes. He'd shown her the door, tears and all, and that was the last time he'd shown any warmth toward anything in skirts.

"What would I do with kids?" he asked. "Look what it's done to Tyson Wade, for God's sake. There he was, a contented bachelor making money hand over fist. He married that model and lost everything—"

"He got everything back, with interest," Lillian interrupted, "and you say one more word about Miss Erin and I'll scald you, so help me!"

He shrugged. "Well, she is pretty. Nice twins, too. They look a little like Ty."

"Poor old thing," Lillian said gently. "He was homely as sin and all alone and meaner than a tickled rattlesnake. And now here he's made his peace with you and even let you have those oil leases you've been after for ten years. Yes sir, love sure is a miracle," she added with a purely calculating look.

He shivered. "Talking about it gives me hives. Talk about something else." He was filling his plate and nibbling between comments.

Lillian folded her hands in front of her, hesitating, but only for an instant. "I've got a problem."

"I know. Grandmother."

"A bigger one."

He stopped eating and looked up. She did seem to be worried. He laid down his fork. "Well? What's the problem?"

She shifted from one foot to the other. "My brother's eldest girl, Marianne," she said. "Ben died last year, you remember."

"Yes. You went to his funeral. His wife died years earlier, didn't she?"

Lillian nodded. "Well, Marianne and her best friend, Beth, went shopping at one of those all-night department store sales. On their way out, as they crossed the parking lot, a man tried to attack them. It was terrible," she continued huskily. "Terrible! The girls were just sickened by the whole experience!" She lowered her voice just enough to sound dramatic. "It left deep scars. Deep emotional scars," she added meaningfully, watching to see how he was reacting. *So far, so good.*

He sat up straighter, listening. "Your niece will be all right, won't she?" he asked hesitantly.

"Yes. She's all right physically." She twisted her skirt. "But it's her state of mind that I'm worried about."

"Marianne..." He nodded, remembering a photograph he'd seen of Lillian's favorite niece. A vivid impression of long dark hair and soft blue eyes and an oval, vulnerable young face brought a momentary smile to his lips.

"She's no raving beauty, and frankly, she hasn't dated very much. Her father was one of those domineering types whose reputation kept the boys away from her when she lived at home. But now..." She sighed even more dramatically. "Poor little Mari." She glanced up. "She's been keeping the books for a big garage. Mostly men. She said it's gotten to the point that if a man comes close enough to open a door for her, she breaks out in a cold sweat. She needs to get away for a little while, out of the city, and get her life back together."

"Poor kid," he said, sincere yet cautious.

"She's almost twenty-two," Lillian said. "What's going to become of her?" she asked loudly, peeking out the corner of her eye at him.

He whistled softly. "Therapy would be her best bet."

"She won't talk to anyone," she said quickly, cocking her head to one side. "Now, I know how you feel about women. I don't even blame you. But I can't turn my back on my own niece." She straightened, playing her trump card. "Now, I'm fully prepared to give up my job and go to her—"

"Oh, for God's sake, you know me better than that after fifteen years," he returned curtly. "Send her an airline ticket."

"She's in Georgia—"

"So what?"

Lillian toyed with a pan of rolls. "Well, thanks. I'll make it up to you somehow," she said with a secretive grin.

"If you're feeling that generous, how about an apple pie?"

The older woman chuckled. "Thirty minutes," she said and dashed off to the kitchen like a woman half her age. She could have danced with glee. He'd fallen for it! Stage one was about to take off! *Forgive me, Mari,* she thought silently and began planning again.

Ward stared after her with confused emotions. He hoped that he'd made the right decision. Maybe he was just going soft in his old age. Maybe . . .

"My bed was more uncomfortable than a sheet filled with cacti," came a harsh, angry old voice from the doorway. He turned as his grandmother ambled in using her cane, broad as a beam and as formidable as a raiding party, all cold green eyes and sagging jowls and champagne-tinted hair that waved around her wide face.

"Why don't you sleep in the stable?" he asked her pleasantly. "Hay's comfortable."

She glared at him and waved her cane. "Shame on you, talking like that to a pitiful old woman!"

"I pity anyone who stands within striking distance of that cane," he assured her. "When do you leave for Galveston?"

"Can't wait to get rid of me, can you?" she demanded as she slid warily into a chair beside him.

"Oh, no," he assured her. "I'll miss you like the plague."

"You cowhand," she grumbled, glaring at him. "Just like your father. He was hell to live with, too."

"You sweet-tempered little woman," he taunted.

"I guess you get that wit from your father. And he got it from me," she confessed. She poured herself a cup of coffee. "I hope Belinda is easier to get along with than you and your saber-toothed housekeeper."

"I am not saber-toothed," Lillian assured her as she brought in more rolls.

"You are so," Mrs. Jessup replied curtly. "In my day we'd have lynched you on a mesquite tree for insubordination!"

"In your day you'd have been hanging beside me," Lillian snorted and walked out.

"Are you going to let her talk to me like that?" Mrs. Jessup demanded of her grandson.

"You surely don't want me to walk into that kitchen alone?" he asked her. "She keeps knives in there." He lowered his voice and leaned toward her. "And a sausage grinder. I've seen it with my own eyes."

Mrs. Jessup tried not to laugh, but she couldn't help herself. She hit at him affectionately. "Reprobate. Why do I put up with you?"

"You can't help yourself," he said with a chuckle. "Eat. You can't travel halfway across Texas on an empty stomach."

She put down her coffee cup. "Are you sure this night flight is a good idea?"

"It's less crowded. Besides, Belinda and her newest boyfriend are going to meet you at the airport," he said. "You'll be safe."

"I guess so." She stared at the platter of beef that was slowly being emptied. "Give me some of that before you gorge yourself!"

"It's my cow," he muttered, green eyes glittering.

"It descended from one of mine. Give it here!"

Ward sighed, defeated. Handing the platter to her with a resigned expression, he watched her beam with the tiny triumph. He had to humor her just a little occasionally. It kept her from getting too crotchety.

Later he drove her to the airport and put her on a plane. As he went back toward his ranch, he wondered about Marianne Raymond and how it was going to be with a young woman around the place getting in his hair. Of course, she was just twenty-two, much too young for him. He was thirty-five now, too old for that kind of child-woman. He shook his head. He only hoped that he'd done the right thing. If he hadn't, things were sure going to be complicated from now on. At one time Lillian's incessant matchmaking had driven him nuts before he'd managed to stop her, though she still harped on his unnatural attitude toward marriage. If only she'd let him alone and stop mothering him! That was the trouble with people who'd worked for you almost half your life, he muttered to himself. They felt obliged to take care of you in spite of your own wishes.

He stared across the pastures at the oil rigs as he eased his elegant white Chrysler onto the highway near Ravine, Texas. His rigs. He'd come a long damned way from the old days spent working on those rigs. His father had dreamed of finding that one big well, but it was Ward who'd done it. He'd borrowed as much as he could and put everything on one big gamble with a friend. And his well had come in. He and the friend had equal shares in it, and they'd long since split up and gone in different directions. When it came to business, Ward Jessup could be ruthless and calculating. He had a shrewd mind and a hard heart, and some of his enemies had been heard to say that he'd foreclose on a starving widow if she owed him money.

That wasn't quite true, but it was close. He'd grown up poor, dirt poor, as his grandmother had good reason to remember. The family had been looked down on for a long time because of Ward's mother. She'd tired of her boring life on the ranch with her two children and had run off with a neighbor's husband, leaving the children for her stunned husband and mother-in-law to raise. Later she'd divorced Ward's father and remarried, but the children had never heard from her again. In a small community like Ravine the scandal had been hard to live down. Worse, just a little later, Ward's father had gone out into the south forty one autumn day with a rifle in his hand and hadn't come home again.

He hadn't left a note or even seemed depressed. They'd found him slumped beside his pickup truck, clutching a piece of ribbon that had belonged to his wife. Ward had never forgotten his father's death, had never forgiven his mother for causing it.

Later, when he'd fallen into Caroline's sweet trap, Ward Jessup had learned the final lesson. These days he had a reputation for breaking hearts, and it wasn't far from the mark. He had come to hate women. Every time he felt tempted to let his emotions show, he remembered his mother and Caroline. And day by day he became even more embittered.

He liked to remember Caroline's face when he'd told her he didn't want her anymore, that he could go on happily all by himself. She'd curled against him with her big black eyes so loving in that face like rice paper and her blond hair cascading like yellow silk down her back. But he'd seen past the beauty to the ugliness, and he never wanted to get that close to a woman again. He'd seen graphically how big a fool the most sensible man could become when a shrewd woman got hold of him. Nope, he told himself. Never again. He'd learned from his mistake. He wouldn't be that stupid a second time.

He pulled into the long driveway of Three Forks and smiled at the live oaks that lined it, thinking of all the history there was in this big, lusty spread of land. He might live and die without an heir, but he'd sure enjoy himself until that time came.

He wondered if Tyson Wade was regretting his decision to lease the pastureland so that Ward could look for the oil that he sensed was there. He and Ty had been enemies for so many years—almost since boyhood—although the reason for all the animosity had long been forgotten in the heat of the continuing battle over property lines, oil rigs and just about everything else.

Ty Wade had changed since his marriage. He'd mellowed, becoming a far cry from the renegade who'd just as soon have started a brawl as talk business. Amazing that a beautiful woman like Erin had agreed to marry the man in the first place. Ty was no pretty boy. In fact, to Ward Jessup, the man looked downright homely. But maybe he had hidden qualities.

Ward grinned at that thought. He wouldn't begrudge his old enemy a little happiness, not since he'd picked up those oil leases that he'd wanted so desperately. It was like a new beginning: making a peace treaty with Tyson Wade and getting his crotchety grandmother out of his hair and off the ranch without bloodshed. He chuckled aloud as he drove back to the house, and it wasn't until he heard the sound that he realized how rarely he laughed these days.

Chapter Two

Marianne Raymond didn't know what to expect when she landed at the San Antonio airport. She knew that Ravine was quite a distance away, and her Aunt Lillian had said that someone would meet her. But what if no one did? Her blue eyes curiously searched the interior of the airport. Aunt Lillian's plea for her to visit had been so unusual, so...odd. Poor old Mr. Jessup, she thought, shaking her head. Poor brave man. Dying of that incurable disease, and Aunt Lillian so determined to make his last days happy. Mari had been delighted to come, to help out. Her vacation was overdue, and the manager of the big garage where she kept the books and wrote the occasional letter had promised that they could do without her for a week or so. Mr. Jessup wanted young people around, he'd told Lillian. Some cheerful company and someone to help him write his memoirs. That would be right up Mari's alley. She'd actually done some feature articles for a local newspaper, and she had literary ambitions, too.

Someday Mari was going to be a novelist. She'd promised herself that. She wrote a portion of her book every night. The story involved a poor city girl who was assaulted by a vicious gang leader and had nightmares about her horrible assailant. She'd told Aunt Lillian the plot over the phone just recently, and the older woman had been delighted with it. Mari wondered about her aunt's sudden enthusiasm because Lillian had never been particularly interested in anything except getting her married off to any likely candidate who came along. After her father's death, especially. The only reason she'd agreed to come down to Ravine was because of poor old Mr. Jessup. At least she could be sure that Aunt Lillian wasn't trying to marry her off to him!

Mari pushed back her hair. It was short now, a twenties-style pageboy with bangs, and it emphasized the rosy oval of her face. She was wearing a simple dropped-waist dress in blue-and-white stripes and carrying only a roly-poly piece of luggage, which contained barely enough clothes to get her through one week.

A tall man attracted her interest, and despite the shyness she felt with most men, she studied him blatantly. He was as big as the side of a barn, tall with rippling muscles and bristling with backcountry masculinity. Wearing a gray suit, an open-necked white shirt and a pearly gray Stetson and boots, he looked big and mean and sexy. The angle of that hat over his black hair was as arrogant as the look on his deeply tanned face, as intimidating as that confident stride that made people get out of his way. He would have made the perfect hero for

Mari's book. The strong, tender man who would lead her damaged heroine back to happiness again...

He didn't look at anyone except Mari, and after a few seconds she realized that he was coming toward her. She clutched the little carryall tightly as he stopped just in front of her, and in spite of her height she had to look up to see his eyes. They were green and cold. Ice-cold.

"Marianne Raymond," he said as if she'd damned well better be. He set her temper smoldering with that confident drawl.

She lifted her chin. "That's right," she replied just as quietly. "Are you from Three Forks Ranch?"

"I *am* Three Forks Ranch," he informed her, reaching for the carryall. "Let's go."

"Not one step," she said, refusing to release it and glaring at him. "Not one single step until you tell me who you are and where we're going."

His eyebrows lifted. They were straight and thick like the lashes over his green eyes. "I'm Ward Jessup," he said. "I'm taking you to your Aunt Lillian." He controlled his temper with a visible effort as he registered her shocked expression and reached for his wallet, flashing it open to reveal his driver's license. "Satisfied?" he drawled and then felt ashamed of himself when he knew why she had reason to be so cautious and nervous of him.

"Yes, thank you," she said. *That* was Ward Jessup? *That* was a dying man? Dazed, she let him take the carryall and followed him out of the airport.

He had a car—a big Chrysler with burgundy leather seats and controls that seemed to do everything, right up to speaking firmly to the passengers about fastening their seat belts.

"I've never seen such an animal," she commented absently as she fastened her seat belt, trying to be a little less hostile. He'd asked for it, but she had to remember the terrible condition that the poor man was in. She felt guilty about her bad manners.

"It's a honey," he remarked, starting the engine. "Have you eaten?"

"Yes, on the plane, thank you," she replied. She folded her hands in her lap and was quiet until they reached the straight open road. The meadows were alive with colorful wildflowers of orange and red and blue, and prickly pear cacti. Mari also noticed long stretches of land where there were no houses and few trees, but endless fences and cattle everywhere.

"I thought there was oil everywhere in Texas," she murmured, staring out at the landscape and the sparse houses.

"What do you think those big metal grasshoppers are?" he asked, glancing at her as he sped down the road.

She frowned. "Oil wells? But where are the big metal things that look like the Eiffel Tower?"

He laughed softly to himself. "My God. Eastern tenderfoot," he chided. "You put up a derrick when you're hunting oil, honey, you don't keep it on stripper wells. Those damned things cost money."

She smiled at him. "I'll bet you weren't born knowing that, either, Mr. Jessup," she said.

"I wasn't." He leaned back and settled his huge frame comfortably.

He sure does look healthy for a dying man, Mari thought absently.

"I worked on rigs for years before I ever owned one."

"That's very dangerous work, isn't it?" she asked conversationally.

"So they say."

She studied his very Roman profile, wondering if anyone had ever painted him. Then she realized that she was staring and turned her attention to the landscape. It was spring and the trees looked misshapen and gloriously soft feathered with leaves.

"What kind of trees are those, anyway?" she asked.

"Mesquite," he said. "It's all over the place at the ranch, but don't ever go grabbing at its fronds. It's got long thorns everywhere."

"Oh, we don't have mesquite in Georgia," she commented, clasping her purse.

"No, just peach trees and magnolia blossoms and dainty little cattle farms."

She glared at him. "In Atlanta we don't have dainty little cattle farms, but we do have a very sophisticated tourism business and quite a lot of foreign investors."

"Don't tangle with me, honey," he advised with a sharp glance. "I've had a hard morning, and I'm just not in the mood for verbal fencing."

"I gave up obeying adults when I became one," she replied.

His eyes swept over her dismissively. "You haven't. Not yet."

"I'll be twenty-two this month," she told him shortly.

"I was thirty-five last month," he replied without looking her way. "And, to me, you'd still be a kid if you were four years older."

"You poor, old, decrepit thing," she murmured under her breath. It was getting harder and harder to feel sorry for him.

"What an interesting houseguest you're going to make, Miss Raymond," he observed as he drove down the interstate. "I'll have to arrange some razor-blade soup to keep your tongue properly sharpened."

"I don't think I like you," she said shortly.

He glared back. "I don't like women," he replied and his voice was as cold as his eyes.

She wondered if he knew why she'd come and decided that Aunt Lillian had probably told him everything. She averted her face to the window and gnawed on her lower lip. She was being deliberately antagonistic, and her upbringing bristled at her lack of manners. He'd asked Lillian to bring her out to Texas; he'd even paid for her ticket. She was supposed to cheer him up, to help him write his memoirs, to make his last days happier. And here she was being rude and unkind and treating him like a bad-tempered old tyrant.

"I'm sorry," she said after a minute.

"What?"

"I'm sorry," she repeated, unable to look at him. "You let me come here, you bought my ticket, and all I've done since I got off the plane is be sarcastic to you. Aunt Lillian told me all about it, you know," she added enigmatically, ignoring the puzzled expression on his face. "I'll do everything I can to make you glad you've brought me here. I'll help you out in every way I can. Well," she amended, "in most ways. I'm not really very comfortable around men," she added with a shy smile.

He relaxed a little, although he didn't smile. His hand caressed the steering wheel as he drove. "That's not hard to understand," he said after a minute, and she guessed that her aunt had told him about her strict upbringing. "But I'm the last man on earth you'd have to worry about in that particular respect. My women know the score, and they aren't that prolific these days. I don't have any interest in girls your age. You're just a baby."

Annoying, unnerving, infuriating man, she thought uncharitably, surprised by his statement. She looked toward him hesitantly, her eyes quiet and steady on his dark face. "Well, I've never had any interest in bad-tempered old men with oil wells," she said with dry humor. "That ought to reassure you as well, Mr. Jessup, sir."

"Don't be cheeky," he murmured with an amused glance. "I'm not that old."

"I'll bet your joints creak," she said under her breath.

He laughed. "Only on cold mornings," he returned. He pulled into the road that led to Three Forks and slowed down long enough to turn and stare into her soft blue eyes. "Tell you what, kid, you be civil to me and I'll be civil to you, and we'll never let people guess what we really think of each other. Okay?"

"Okay," she returned, eager to humor him. Poor man!

His green eyes narrowed. "Pity, about your age and that experience," he commented, letting his gaze wander over her face. "You're uncommon. Like your aunt."

"My aunt is the reincarnation of General Patton," she said. She wondered what experience he meant. "She could win wars if they'd give her a uniform."

"I'll amen that," he said.

"Thanks for driving up to get me," she added. "I appreciate it."

"I didn't know how you'd feel about a strange cowboy," he said gently. "Although we don't know each other exactly, I knew that Lillian's surely mentioned me and figured you'd be a bit more comfortable."

"I was." She didn't tell him how Lillian had described him as Attila the Hun in denim and leather.

"Don't tell her we've been arguing," he said unexpectedly as he put the car back in gear and drove up to the house. "It'll upset her. She stammered around for a half hour and even threatened to quit before she got up the nerve to suggest your visit."

"Bless her old heart." Mari sighed, feeling touched. "She's quite a lady, my aunt. She really cares about people."

"Next to my grandmother, she's the only woman that I can tolerate under my roof."

"Is your grandmother here?" she asked as they reached a huge cedarwood house with acres of windows and balconies.

"She left last week, thank God," he said heavily. "One more day of her and I'd have left and so would Lillian. She's too much like me. We only get along for short stretches."

"I like your house," she remarked as he opened the door for her.

"I don't, but when the old one burned down, my sister was going with an architect who gave us a good bid." He glared at the house. "I thought he was a smart boy. He turned out to be one of those innovative New Wave builders who like to experiment. The damned bathrooms have sunken tubs and Jacuzzis, and there's an indoor stream... Oh, God, what a nightmare of a house if you sleepwalk! You could drown in the living room or be swept off into the river."

She couldn't help laughing. He sounded horrified. "Why didn't you stop him?" she asked.

"I was in Canada for several months," he returned. He didn't elaborate. This strange woman didn't need to know that he'd gone into the wilderness to heal after Caroline's betrayal and that he hadn't cared what replaced the old house after lightning had struck and set it afire during a storm.

"Well, it's not so bad," she began but was interrupted when Lillian exploded out of the house, arms outstretched. Mari ran into them, feeling safe for the first time in weeks.

"Oh, you look wonderful," Lillian said with a sigh. "How are you? How was the trip?"

"I'm fine, and it was very nice of Mr. Jessup to come and meet me," she said politely. She turned, nodding toward him. "Thanks again. I hope the trip didn't tire you too much?"

"What?" he asked blankly.

"I told Mari how hard you'd been working lately, boss," Lillian said quickly. "Come on, honey, let's go inside!"

"I'll bring the bag," Ward said curiously and followed them into the rustic but modern house.

Mari loved it. It was big and rambling and there was plenty of room everywhere. It was just the house for an outdoorsman, right down to the decks that overlooked the shade trees around the house.

"I think this place is perfect for Ward, but for heaven's sake, don't tell him that! And please don't let on that you know about his condition," Lillian added, her eyes wary. "You didn't say anything about it?" she asked, showing Mari through the ultramodern upstairs where her bedroom overlooked the big pool below and the flat landscape beyond, fenced and cross-fenced with milling cattle.

"Oh, no, Scout's honor," Mari said. "But how am I going to help him write his memoirs?"

"We'll work up to it in good time," Lillian assured her. "He, uh, didn't ask why you came?"

Mari sighed. "He seemed to think I'd asked to come. Odd man, he thought I was afraid of him. Me, afraid of men, isn't that a scream? Especially after what Beth and I did at that all-night department store."

"Don't ever tell him, please," Lillian pleaded. "It would...upset him. We mustn't do that," she added darkly. "It could be fatal!"

"I won't, truly I won't," Mari promised. "He sure is healthy looking for a dying man, isn't he?"

"Rugged," Lillian said. "Real rugged. He'd never let on that he was in pain."

"Poor brave man," Mari said with a sigh. "He's so tough."

Lillian grinned as she turned away.

"Did his sister like this house?" Mari asked later after she'd unpacked and was helping Lillian in the kitchen.

"Oh, yes," Lillian confided to her niece. "But the boss hates it!"

"Is his sister like him?" Mari asked.

"To look at, no. But in temperament, definitely," the older woman told her. "They're both high-strung and mean tempered."

"You mentioned that he had a male secretary," Mari reminded her as she rolled out a piecrust.

"Yes. David Meadows. He's young and very efficient, but he doesn't like being called a secretary." Lillian grinned. "He thinks he's an administrative assistant."

"I'll have to remember that."

"I don't know what the boss would do without him, either," Lillian continued as she finished quartering the apples for the pie. Another apple pie might soften him up a little, she was thinking. "David keeps everything running smoothly around here, from paying the accounts to answering the phone and scheduling appointments. The boss stays on the road most of the time, closing deals. The oil business is vast these days. Last week he was in Saudi Arabia. Next week he's off to South America."

"All that traveling must get tiresome," Mari said, her blue eyes curious. "Isn't it dangerous for him in his condition?"

For a moment Lillian looked hunted. Then she brightened. "Oh, no, the doctor says it's actually good for him. He takes it easy, and it keeps his mind off things. He never talks about it, though. He's a very private person."

"He seems terribly cold," Mari remarked thoughtfully.

"Camouflage," Lillian assured her. "He's warm and gentle and a prince of a man," she added. "A prince! Now, get this pie fixed, girl. You make the best pies I've ever tasted, even better than my own."

"Mama taught me," Mari said gently. "I really miss her sometimes. Especially in the autumn. We used to go up into the mountains to see the leaves. Dad was always too busy, but Mama and I were adventurous. It's been eight years since she died. And only one since Dad went. I'm glad I still have you."

Lillian tried not to look touched, but she was. "Get busy," she said gruffly, turning away. "It isn't good to look back."

That was true, Mari thought, keeping her own thoughts on the present instead of the past. She felt sad about Ward Jessup—even if he was a dreadful oilman. She'd heard her aunt talk about him for so many years that she felt as if she knew him already. If only she could make it through the week without making him angry or adding to his problems. She just wanted to help him, if he'd let her.

Mari was just going into the other room to call him when her attention was caught by the stream running through the room, lit by underwater colored lights. It was eerie and beautiful indoor "landscaping," with plants everywhere and literally a stream running through the middle of the living room, wide enough to swim in.

Not paying much attention to where she was going, Mari backed along the carpet, only half aware of footsteps, and suddenly collided with something warm and solid.

There was a terribly big splash and a furious curse. When she turned around, she felt herself go pale.

"Oh, Mr. Jessup, I'm sorry," she wailed, burying her cheeks in her hands.

He was very wet. Not only was he soaked, but there was a lily pad on top of his straight black hair that had been slicked down by all the water. He was standing, and though the water came to his chin, he looked very big and very angry. As he sputtered and blinked, Mari noticed that his green eyes were exactly the shade of the lily pad.

"Damn you..." he began as he moved toward the carpeted "shore" with a dangerous look on his dark face. At that moment nobody would have guessed that he was a dying man. As quick as lightning he was out of the water, dripping on the carpet. Suddenly Mari forgot his delicate condition and ran like hell.

"Aunt Lillian!"

Mari ran for the kitchen as fast as her slender legs could carry her, a blur in jeans and a white sweatshirt as she darted down the long hall toward the relative safety of the kitchen.

Behind her, soggy footsteps and curses followed closely.

"Aunt Lillian, help!" she cried as she dashed through the swing door.

She forgot that swing doors tend to swing back when forcibly opened by hysterical people. It slammed back into a tall, wet, cursing man. There was an ominous thud and the sound of shattering ceramic pieces.

Lillian looked at her niece in wide-eyed shock. "Oh, Mari," she said. Her ears told her more than she wanted to know as she stared at the horrified face of her niece. "Oh, Mari."

"I think Mr. Jessup may need a little help, Aunt Lillian," Mari began hesitantly.

"Prayer might be more beneficial at the moment, dear," Aunt Lillian murmured nervously. She wiped her hands on her printed apron and cautiously opened the swing door to peer into the dining room.

Ward Jessup was just sitting up among the ruins of his table setting, china shards surrounding him. His suit was wet, and there was a puddle of water under him as he tugged his enormous frame off the floor. His eyes were blazing in a face that had gone ruddy in anger. He held on to a chair and rose slowly, glaring at Lillian's half-hidden face with an expression that told her there was worse to come.

"She's really a nice girl, boss," Lillian began, "once you get to know her."

He brushed back his soaked hair with a lean, angry hand, and his chest rose and fell heavily. "I have a meeting just after supper," he said. "I sent the rest of my suits to the cleaner's this afternoon. This is the last suit I had. I didn't expect to go swimming in it."

"We could dry it and I could...press it," Lillian suggested halfheartedly, pretty sure that she couldn't do either.

"I could forget the whole damned thing, too," he said curtly. He glared at Lillian. "Nothing is going to make up for this, you know."

She swallowed. "How about a nice freshly baked apple pie with ice cream?"

He tilted his head to one side and pursed his lips. "Freshly baked?"

"Freshly baked."

"With ice cream?"

"That's right," she promised.

He shrugged his wet shoulders. "I'll think about it." He turned and sloshed off down the hall.

Lillian leaned back against the wall and stared at her transfixed niece. "Honey," she said gently, "would you like to tell me what happened?"

"I don't know," Mari burst out. "I went in to call him to the table, and I started looking at that beautiful artificial stream, and the next thing I knew, he'd fallen into it. I must have, well, backed into him."

"How you could miss a man his size is beyond me." Lillian shook her head and grabbed a broom and dustpan from the closet.

"I had my back to him, you know."

"I wouldn't ever do that again after this if I were you," the older woman advised. "If it wasn't for that apple pie, even I couldn't save you!"

"Yes, ma'am," Mari said apologetically. "Oh, Aunt Lillian, that poor, brave man." She sighed. "I hope he doesn't get a chill because of me. I'd never be able to live with myself!"

"There, there," Lillian assured her, "he's tough, you know. He'll be fine. For now, I mean," she added quickly.

Mari covered her face with her hands in mingled relief and suppressed amusement. Ward Jessup was quite a man. How sad that he had such little time left. She didn't think she'd ever forget the look on his face when he climbed out of the indoor stream, or the excited beat of her heart as she'd run from him. It was new to be chased by a man, even an ill one, and exhilarating to be uninhibited in one's company. She'd been shy with men all her life, but she didn't feel shy with Ward. She felt...*feminine*. And that was as new to her as the rapid beat of her heart.

Chapter Three

I didn't mean to knock you into the pool," Mari told Ward the minute he entered the dining room.

He stopped in the doorway and stared at her from his great height. His hair was dry now, thick and straight against his broad forehead, and his wet clothes had been exchanged for dry jeans and a blue plaid shirt. His green eyes were a little less hostile than they had been minutes before.

"It isn't a pool," he informed her. "It's an indoor stream. And next time, Miss Raymond, I'd appreciate it if you'd watch where the hell you're going."

"Yes, sir," she said quickly.

"I told you not to let him put that stream in the living room," Lillian gloated.

He glared at her. "Keep talking and I'll give you an impromptu swimming lesson."

"Yes, boss." She turned on her heel and went back into the kitchen to fetch the rest of the food.

"I really am sorry," Mari murmured.

"So am I," he said unexpectedly, and his green eyes searched hers quietly. "I hope I didn't frighten you."

She glanced down at her shoes, nervous of the sensations that his level gaze prompted. "It's hard to be afraid of a man with a lily pad on his head."

"Stop that," he grumbled, jerking out a chair.

"You might consider putting up guardrails," she suggested dryly as she sat down across from him, her blue eyes twinkling with the first humor she'd felt in days.

"You'd better keep a life jacket handy," he returned.

She stuck her tongue out at him impulsively and watched his thick eyebrows arch.

He shook out his napkin with unnecessary force and laid it across his powerful thighs. "My God, you're living dangerously," he told her.

"I'm not afraid of you," she said smartly and meant it.

"That isn't what your Aunt Lillian says," he observed with narrowed eyes.

She stared at him blankly. "I beg your pardon?"

"She says you're afraid of men," he continued. He scowled at her puzzled expression. "Because of what happened to you and your friend," he prompted.

She blinked, wondering what her aunt had told him about that. After all, having your purse pinched by an overweight juvenile delinquent wasn't really enough to terrify most women. Especially when she and Beth had run the offender down, beaten the stuffing out of him, recovered the purse and sat on him until the police got there.

"You know, dear," Lillian blustered as she came through the door, shaking her head and smiling all at once. She looked as red as a beet, too. "The horrible experience you had!"

"Horrible?" Mari asked.

"Horrible!" Lillian cried. "We can't talk about it now!"

"We can't?" Mari parroted blankly.

"Not at the table. Not in front of the boss!" She jerked her head curtly toward him two or three times.

"Have you got a crick in your neck, Aunt Lillian?" her niece asked with some concern.

"No, dear, why do you ask? Here! Have some fried chicken and some mashed potatoes!" She shoved dishes toward her niece and began a monologue that only ended when it was time for dessert.

"I think something's wrong with Aunt Lillian," Mari confided to Ward the moment Lillian started back into the kitchen for the coffeepot.

"Yes, so do I," he replied. "She's been acting strangely for the past few days. Don't let on you know. We'll talk later."

She nodded, concerned. Lillian was back seconds later, almost as if she was afraid to leave them alone together. How strange.

"Well, I think I'll go up to bed," Mari said after she finished her coffee, glancing quickly at Aunt Lillian. "I'm very tired."

"Good idea," Ward said. "You get some rest."

"Yes," Lillian agreed warmly. "Good night, dear."

She bent to kiss her aunt. "See you in the morning, Aunt Lillian," she murmured and glanced at Ward. "Good night, Mr. Jessup."

"Good night, Miss Raymond," he said politely.

Mari went quietly upstairs and into her bedroom. She sat by the window and looked down at the empty swimming pool with its wooden privacy fence and the gently rolling, brush-laden landscape, where cattle moved lazily and a green haze heralded spring. Minutes later there was a stealthy knock at the door, and Ward Jessup came into the room, scowling.

"Want me to leave the door open?" he asked hesitantly.

She stared at him blankly. "Why? Are you afraid I might attack you?"

He stared back. "Well, after the experience you had, I thought..."

"What experience?" she asked politely.

"The man at the shopping center," he said, his green eyes level and frankly puzzled as he closed the door behind him.

"Are you afraid of me because of that?" she burst out. "I do realize you may be a little weak, Mr. Jessup, but I promise I won't hurt you!"

He gaped at her. "What?"

"You don't have to be afraid of me," she assured him. "I'm not really as bad as Aunt Lillian made me sound, I'm sure. And it's only a red belt, after all, not a black one. I only sat on him until the police came. I hardly even bruised him—"

"Whoa," he said curtly. He cocked his dark head and peered at her. "You sat on him?"

"Sure," she agreed, pushing her hair out of her eyes. "Didn't she tell you that Beth and I ran the little weasel down to get my purse back and beat the stuffing out of him? Overweight little juvenile delinquent, he was lucky I didn't skin him alive."

"You weren't attacked?" he persisted.

"Well, sort of." She shrugged. "He stole my purse. He couldn't have known I was a karate student."

"Oh, my God," he burst out. His eyes narrowed, his jaw tautened. "That lying old turkey!"

"How dare you call my aunt a turkey!" she returned hotly. "After all she's doing for you?"

"What, exactly, is she doing for me?"

"Well, bringing me here, to help you write your memoirs before...the end," she faltered. "She told me all about your incurable illness—"

"Incurable illness?" he bellowed.

"You're dying," she told him.

"Like hell I am," he said fiercely.

"You don't have to act brave and deny it," she replied hesitantly. "She told me that you wanted young people around to cheer you up. And somebody to help you write your memoirs. I'm going to be a novelist one day," she added. "I want to be a writer."

"Good. You can practice with your aunt's obituary," he muttered, glaring toward the door.

"You can't do that to a helpless old lady," she began.

"Watch me." He was heading for the door, his very stride frightening.

"Oh, no! You can't!" She ran after him, got in front of him and plastered herself against the door. "You'll have to go through me."

"Suits me, Joan of Arc," he grumbled, catching her by the waist. He lifted her clear off the floor until she was unnervingly at eye level with him. "You sweet little angel of mercy, you."

"Put me down or I'll...I'll put you down," she threatened.

He stared amusedly into her blue eyes under impossibly thick lashes. "Will you? Go ahead. Show me how you earned that red belt."

She tried. She used every trick her instructor had taught her, and all it accomplished was to leave her dangling from his powerful hands, panting into his mocking smile.

"Had enough?" she huffed.

"Not at all. Aren't you finished yet?" he asked politely.

She aimed one more kick, which he blocked effortlessly. She sagged in his powerful hold. Lord, he was strong! "Okay," she said, sighing wearily. "Now I'm finished."

"Next time," he told her as he put her back on her feet, leaving his hands tightly around her waist, "make sure your intended victim didn't take the same course of study. My belt is black. Tenth degree."

"Damn you!" she cursed sharply.

"And we'll have no more of that in this house," he said shortly, emphasizing the angry remark with a reproachful slap to her bottom, nodding as she gasped in outrage. "You've been working in that garage for too long already, if that's any example of what you're being taught."

"I'm not a child!" she retorted. "I'm an adult!"

"No, you aren't," he replied, jerking her against him with a mocking smile. "But maybe I can help you grow up a little."

He bent his head and found her lips with a single smooth motion, pressing her neck back against his muscular shoulder with the fierce possessiveness of his hard mouth.

Mari thought that in all her life nothing so unexpected had ever happened to her. His lips were warm and hard and insistent, forcing hers open so that he could put the tip of his tongue just under them, his breath tasting of coffee and mint, the strength of his big body overwhelming her with its hard warmth.

For an instant she tried to struggle, only to find herself enveloped in his arms, wrapped up against him so tightly that she could hardly breathe. And everywhere her face turned, his was there, his mouth provocative, sensuous, biting at hers, doing the most intimate things to it.

Her legs felt funny. They began to tremble as they came into sudden and shocking contact with his. Her heart raced. Her body began to ache with heat and odd longings. Her breath caught somewhere in her chest, and her breasts felt swollen. Because these new sensations frightened her, she tried to struggle. But he only held her tighter, not brutally but firmly, and went on kissing her.

His fingers were in her hair, tugging gently, strong and warm at her nape as they turned her face where he wanted it. His mouth pressed roughly against hers and opened softly, teaching hers. Eventually the drugging sweetness of it took the fight out of her. With a tiny sigh she began to relax.

"Open your mouth, Mari," he murmured in a deep, rough whisper, punctuating the command with a sensual brushing of his open lips against hers.

She obeyed him without hearing him, her body with a new heat, her hands searching over his arms to find hard muscle and warm strength through the fabric. She wanted to touch his skin, to experience every hard line of him. She wanted to open his shirt and touch his chest and see if the wiry softness she could feel through it was thick hair....

Her abandon shocked her back to reality. Her eyes opened and she tugged at his arms, only vaguely aware of the sudden, fierce hunger in his mouth just before he felt her resistance. He lifted his head, taking quick, short breaths, and by the time her eyes opened, he was back in control.

He was watching her, half amused, half mocking. He lifted his mouth, breathing through his nose, and let her move away.

"You little virgin," he accused in a tone that she didn't recognize. "You don't even know how to make love."

Her swollen lips could barely form words. She had to swallow and try twice to make herself heard. "That wasn't fair," she said finally.

"Why not?" he asked. "You tried to kick me, didn't you?"

"That isn't the way...a gentleman gets even," she said, still panting.

"I'm no gentleman," he assured her, smiling even with those cold green eyes. The smile grew colder as he realized how close he'd come to letting her knock him off balance physically. She was dangerous. Part of him wanted her off the property. But another part was hungry for more of that innocently ardent response he'd won from her. His own emotions confused him. "Haven't you realized yet why you're here, Georgia peach?" he asked mockingly. And when she shook her head, he continued, half amused. "Aunt Lillian is matchmaking. She wants you to marry me."

Mari's pupils dilated. "Marry you!"

His back stiffened. She didn't have to make it sound like the rack, did she? He glared down at her. "Well, plenty have wanted to, let me tell you," he muttered.

"Masochists," she shot back, humiliated by her aunt, his attitude and that unexpectedly ardent attack just minutes before. "Anyway," she said salvaging her pride, "Aunt Lillian would never—"

"She did." He studied her with a cold smile. "But I'm too old for you and too jaded. And I don't want to risk my heart again. So go home. Fast."

"It can't be fast enough to suit me. Honest," she told him huskily as she tried to catch her breath. "I don't want to wake up shackled to a man like you."

"How flattering of you."

"I want a partner, not a possessor," she said shakily. "I thought I knew something about men until just now. I don't know anything at all. And I'll be delighted to go back home and join a convent!"

"Was it that bad?" he taunted.

"You scare me, big man," she said and meant it. She backed away from him. "I'll stick to my own age group from now on, thanks. I'll bet you've forgotten more about making love than I'll ever learn."

He smiled slowly, surprised by her frankness. "I probably have. But you're pretty sweet all the same."

"Years too young for a renegade like you."

"I could be tempted," he murmured thoughtfully.

"I couldn't. You'd seduce me and leave me pregnant, and Aunt Lillian would quit, and I'd have to go away and invent a husband I didn't have, and our child would grow up never knowing his father..." she burst out.

His eyes widened. He actually chuckled. "My God, what an imagination."

"I told you I wanted to be a writer," she reminded him. "And now, since you're not dying, would you mind leaving me to pack? I think I can be out of here in ten minutes."

"She'll be heartbroken," he said unexpectedly.

"That's not my problem."

"She's your aunt. Of course it's your problem," he returned. "You can't possibly leave now. She'd—"

"Oh!"

The cry came from downstairs. They looked at each other and both dived for the door, opening it just in time to find Lillian on her back on the bottom step, groaning, one leg in an unnatural position.

Mari rushed down the stairs just behind Ward. "Oh, Aunt Lillian!" she wailed, staring at the strained old face with its pasty complexion. "How could you do this to me?"

"To you?" Lillian bit off, groaning again. "Child, it's my leg!"

"I was going to leave—" Mari began.

"Leave the dishes for you, no doubt." Ward jumped in with a warning glance in Mari's direction. "Isn't that right, Miss Raymond?" Fate was working for him as usual, he mused. Now he'd have a little time to find out just why this woman disturbed him so much. And to get her well out of his system, one way or another, before she left. He had to prove to himself that Mari wasn't capable of doing to him what Caroline had done. It was a matter of male pride.

Mari swallowed, wondering whether to go along with Ward. He did look pretty threatening. And huge. "Uh, that's right. The dishes. But I can do them!" she added brightly.

"It looks like . . . you may be doing them . . . for quite a while, if you . . . don't mind," Lillian panted between groans while Wade rushed to the telephone and dialed the emergency service number.

"You poor darling." Mari sighed, holding Lillian's wrinkled hand. "What happened?"

"I missed Ward and wondered if he might be...if you might be . . ." She cleared her throat and stared at Mari through layers of pain. "You didn't say anything to him?" she asked quickly. "About his . . . condition?"

Mari bit her tongue. *Forgive me for lying, Lord,* she thought. She crossed her fingers behind her. "Of course not," she assured her aunt with a blank smile. "He was just telling me about the ranch."

"Thank God." Lillian sank back. "My leg's broken, you know," she bit off. She glanced up as Ward rejoined them, scowling down at her. She forced a pitiful smile. "Well, boss, I guess you'll have to send for your grandmother," she said slyly.

He glared at her. "Like hell! I just got her off the place! Anyway, why should I?" he continued, bending to hold her other hand. "Your niece won't mind a little cooking, will she?" he added with a pointed glance at Mari.

Mari shifted restlessly. "Well, actually—"

"Of course she won't." Lillian grinned and then grimaced. "Will you, darling? You need to...recuperate." She chose her words carefully. "From your bad experience," she added, jerking her head toward Ward, her eyes pleading with her niece. "You know, at the shopping center?"

"Oh. That bad experience." Mari nodded, glancing at Ward and touching her lower lip where it was slightly swollen.

A corner of his mouth curved up and his eyes twinkled. "It wasn't that bad, was it?" he murmured.

"It was terrible!" Lillian broke in.

"You said it," Mari agreed blithely, her blue eyes accusing. "Besides, I thought you couldn't wait to push me out the door."

"You want her to leave?" Lillian wailed.

"No, I don't want her to leave," Ward said with suffering patience. He lifted his chin and stared down his straight nose at Mari, then smiled. "I've got plans for her," he added in a tone that was a threat in itself.

That was what bothered Mari. Now she was trapped by Lillian's lies and Ward's allegiance to his housekeeper. She wondered what on earth she was going to do, caught between the two of them, and she wondered why Ward Jessup wanted her to stay. He hated women most of the time, from what Lillian had divulged about him. He wasn't a marrying man, and he was a notorious womanizer. Surely he wouldn't try to seduce her. Would he?

She stared at him over Lillian's supine form with troubled eyes. He had an unscrupulous reputation. She wasn't so innocent that she hadn't recognized that evident hunger in his hard mouth just before she'd started fighting him.

But his green eyes mocked her, dared her, challenged her. She'd stay, he told himself. He'd coax her into it. Then he could find some way to make her show her true colors. He was betting there was a little of Caroline's makeup in her, too. She was just another female despite her innocence. She was a woman, and all women were unscrupulous and calculating. If he could make her drop the disguise, if he could prove she was just like all the other she-cats, he could rid himself of his unexpected lust. Lust, of course, was all it was. He forgave Lillian for her fall. It was going to work right in with his plans. Yes, it was.

Chapter Four

Lillian was comfortably settled in a room in the small Ravine hospital. The doctor had ordered a series of tests—not because of her broken leg but because of her blood pressure reading taken in the emergency room.

"Will she be all right, do you think?" Mari asked Ward as they waited for the doctor to speak to them. For most of the evening they'd been sitting in this waiting room. Ward paced and drank black coffee while Mari just stared into space worriedly. Lillian was her last living relative. Without the older woman she'd be all alone.

"She's tough," Ward said noncommittally. He glared at his watch. "My God, I hate waiting! I almost wish I smoked so that I'd have something to help kill the time."

"You don't smoke?" Mari said with surprise.

"Never could stand the things," he muttered. "Clogging up my lungs with smoke never seemed sensible."

Her eyebrows lifted. "But you drink."

"Not to excess," he returned, glancing down at her. "I like whiskey and water once in a blue moon, and I'll take a drink of white wine. But I won't do it and drive." He grinned. "All those commercials got to me. Those crashing beer glasses stick in my mind."

She smiled back a little shyly. "I don't drink at all."

"I guess not, tenderfoot," he murmured. "You aren't old enough to need to."

"My dad used to say that it isn't the age, it's the mileage."

His eyebrows arched. "How much mileage do you have, lady?" he taunted. "You look and feel pretty green to me."

Her face colored furiously, and she hated that knowing look on his dark face. "Listen here, Mr. Jessup—"

"Mr. Jessup." His name was echoed by a young resident physician, who came walking up in a white coat holding a clipboard. He shook hands with Ward and nodded as he was introduced tersely to Mari.

"She'll be all right," he told the two brusquely. "But I'd like to keep her one more day and run some more tests. She's furious, but I think it's for the best. Her blood pressure was abnormally high when we admitted her and it still is. I think that she might have had a slight stroke and that it caused her fall."

Mari had sudden horrible visions and went pale. "Oh, no," she whispered.

"I said, I think," the young doctor emphasized and then smiled. "She might have lost her balance for a number of reasons. That's why I want to run the tests.

Even a minor ear infection or sinusitis could have caused it. I want to know for sure. But one thing's certain, and that's her attitude toward the high blood pressure medication she hasn't been taking."

Ward and Mari exchanged puzzled glances. "I wasn't aware that she had high blood pressure medication," Ward said.

"I guessed that," the young doctor said ruefully. "She was diagnosed a few weeks ago by Dr. Bradley. She didn't even get the prescription filled." He sighed. "She seems to look upon it as a death sentence, which is absurd. It's not, if she just takes care of herself."

"She will from now on," Mari promised. "If I have to roll the pills up in steak and trick them into her."

The young resident grinned from ear to ear. "You have pets?"

"I used to have a cat," Mari confided. "And the only way I could get medicine into him was by tricking him. Short of rolling him up in a towel."

Ward glared at her. "That's no way to treat a sick animal."

She lifted her thin eyebrows. "And how would you do it?"

"Force his mouth open and shove the pills down his throat, of course," he said matter-of-factly. "Before you say it," he added when her mouth opened, "try rolling a half-ton bull in a towel!"

The young doctor covered his mouth while Mari glared up at the taciturn oilman.

"I'll get the pills into her, regardless," Mari assured the doctor. She glanced at Ward Jessup. "And it won't be by having them forced down her throat like a half-ton bull!"

"When will you know something?" Ward asked.

"I'll have the tests by early afternoon, and I'll confer with Dr. Bradley. If you can be here about four o'clock, I'll have something to tell you," the young man said.

"Thank you, Doctor...?"

"Jackson," he replied, smiling. "And don't worry too much," he told Mari. "She's a strong-willed woman. I'd bet on her."

They stopped by Lillian's room and found her half sedated, fuming and glaring as she sat propped up in bed.

"Outrageous!" Lillian burst out the minute they entered the room. "They won't give back my clothes. They're making me spend the night in this icebox, and they won't feed me or give me a blanket!"

"Now, now." Mari laughed gently and bent to kiss the thin face. "You're going to be fine. They said so. They just want to run a few more tests. You'll be out of here in no time."

That reassured the older woman a little, but her beady black eyes went to Ward for reassurance. He wouldn't lie to her. Not him. "Am I all right?" she asked.

"You might have had a stroke," he said honestly, ignoring Mari's shocked glare. "They want to find out."

Lillian sighed. "I figured that. I sure did. Well," she said, brightening, "you two will have to get along without me for a day or so." That seemed to cheer her up, too. Her eyes twinkled at the thought of them alone together in the house.

Ward could read her mind. He wanted to wring her neck, too, but he couldn't hurt a sick lady. First he had to get her well.

"I'll take good care of baby sister, here," he said, nodding toward Mari, and grinned.

Lillian's face fell comically. "She's not that young," she faltered.

"Aunt Lillian!" Mari said, outraged. "Remember my horrible experience!"

"Oh, that." Lillian nibbled her lip. "Oh. That!" She cleared her throat, her eyes widened. "Well . . ."

"I'll help her get over it," Ward promised. He glanced down at Mari. "She's offered to help me get some of my adventures in the oil business down on paper. Wasn't that nice? And on her vacation, too," he added.

Lillian brightened. *Good.* They weren't talking about his "fatal illness" or her "brutal attack." With any luck they wouldn't stumble onto the truth until they were hooked on each other! She actually smiled. "Yes, how sweet of you, Mari!"

Although Mari felt like screaming, she smiled at her aunt. "Yes. Well, I thought it would give me something interesting to do. In between cooking and cleaning and such."

Lillian frowned. "I'm really sorry about this," she said, indicating her leg.

"Get well," Ward said shortly. "Don't be sorry. And one more thing. Whether or not this fall was caused by your blood pressure, you're taking those damned pills from now on. I'm going to ride herd on you like a fanatical ramrod on a trail drive. Got that?"

"Yes, sir, boss," Lillian said, pleased by his concern. She hadn't realized she mattered so much to anyone. Even Mari seemed worried. "I'll be fine. And I'll do what they tell me."

"Good for you," Ward replied. He cocked his head. "They said it could have been an ear infection or sinusitis, too. So don't go crazy worrying about a stroke. Did you black out before you went down?" he persisted.

Lillian sighed. "Not completely. I just got real dizzy."

He smiled "That's reassuring."

"I hope so. Now, you two go home," Lillian muttered. "Let me sleep. Whatever they gave me is beginning to work with a vengeance." She closed her eyes as they said their goodbyes, only to open them as they started to leave. "Mari, he likes his eggs scrambled with a little milk in them," she said. "And don't make the coffee too weak."

"I'll manage," Mari promised. "Just get well. You're all I have."

"I know." Lillian sighed as they closed the door behind them. "That's what worries me so."

But they didn't hear that troubled comment. Mari was fuming all the way to the car.

"You shouldn't have told her what the doctor said." She glowered at him as they drove out of the parking lot.

"You don't know her very well," he returned. He pulled into the traffic without blinking. Ravine had grown in the past few years, and the traffic was growing with it, but speeding cars didn't seem to bother him.

"She's my aunt. Of course I know her!"

"She isn't the kind of woman you nurse along," he shot back. "Any more than I'm that kind. I like the truth, even if it hurts, and so does she. You don't do people any favors by hiding it. You only make the impact worse when it comes out. God, I hate lies. There's nothing on earth I hate more."

He probably had a good reason for that attitude, but Mari wasn't going to pry into his privacy by asking.

At least now she understood Aunt Lillian's matchmaking frenzy. If the older woman had expected to die, she might also have worried about Mari's future. But to try to give Mari to a man like the one beside her was almost criminal! The very thought of being tied to that ex-drill rigger made her blanche. He frightened her in a way no other man ever had. It wasn't fear of brutality or even of rough behavior. It was fear of involvement, of being led on and dumped, the way Johnny Greenwood had teased her and taken her places, and then when she was drunk on loving him, he'd announced his engagement to someone else.

Ward Jessup wasn't the man for marriage, but he wouldn't mind amusing himself with a woman and then dropping her. He seemed to hate women, to be spoiling for revenge on the entire sex. She remembered him saying that he could only tolerate his grandmother and Lillian under his roof, and that said it all. She'd have to be very careful not to fall under his spell. Because he was just playing, and she didn't even know the first thing about his game.

She went to her room as soon as they were back at Three Forks, and although she hated her vulnerability, she actually locked her bedroom door. Not that he'd try anything, she assured herself. But, just in case, a little precaution wouldn't hurt.

The next morning she was awake at dawn. Rather than lie in bed and worry about Aunt Lillian, she got up, dressed in jeans and a yellow pullover and went to cook the beast's breakfast.

She did love this house, indoor waterway and all. It seemed to catch and scatter light so that the darkest corner was bright and cheery. The kitchen reflected the rest of the house. It was spacious and cheerful and contained every modern appliance known to man.

She started the coffee maker and fried bacon. By the time the aroma of coffee was filling the kitchen, she had biscuits in the oven and was setting the big, elegant dining room table.

"What the hell are you doing that for?" Ward Jessup asked from the doorway. "I don't mind eating in the kitchen."

She jumped, turning in time to see him shrug into a chambray shirt. His chest was...incredible. She couldn't help but stare. Despite her age and her exposure to men at the garage where she worked, she'd never in her life seen anything like Ward Jessup without his shirt. Talk about masculine perfection! His chest was as tanned as his face. Broad, rippling with muscle, tapering to his belt, it had a perfect wedge of dark, thick hair that made Mari's jaw drop.

"Close your mouth, honey, you'll catch flies that way," he said, then chuckled, torn between exasperation and honest flattery at her rapt and explicit stare.

She turned back to her table setting with trembling fingers, hating her youth and inexperience, hating the big man who was making fun ot it. "Excuse me. I'm not used to men...half dressed like that."

"Then you should have seen me ten minutes ago, sprout, before I got up. I sleep in the raw."

Now Mari was sure she was blushing. She pursed her lips as she put silverware at their places.

He came up behind her so that she could feel the heat of his big body and took her gently by the shoulders. "That wasn't fair, was it?" he murmured.

"No," she agreed, "considering what a beautiful breakfast I just fixed you."

His lips tugged into a smile. "Do I smell bacon?"

"And biscuits and an omelette and hash brown potatoes and hot coffee," she continued, glancing up at him.

"Then what are you standing here for?" he asked. "Feed me!"

She was rapidly becoming convinced that his appetite was the great love of his life. Food could stop his temper dead, keep him from teasing and prevent homicide, as that apple pie had done after she'd knocked him into the water. It was useful to have such a weapon, when dealing with such a formidable enemy, she thought as she went to put the platters on the table.

He ate without talking, and he didn't sit and read a newspaper, as her father always had done in her youth. She watched him curiously.

His eyebrows shot up. "Something bothering you?"

"Not really." She laughed self-consciously. "It's just that the only man I've ever had breakfast with was my father, and he read his paper all through it."

"I don't read at the table," he said. He finished his last mouthful of biscuit, washed it down with coffee and poured himself a second cup from the carafe. Then he sat back in his chair and stared straight into Mari's eyes. "Why does my chest disturb you?"

She tingled from her head to her toes at the unexpected question and felt a wave of heat wash over her. Some old lines about fighting fire with fire shot into her mind. "Because it's beautiful, in a purely masculine way," she blurted out.

He pondered that for a minute before he smiled into his coffee. "You don't lie well, do you?"

"I think it's a waste of time," she replied. She got to her feet. "If you're through, I'll clear the table."

She started to pick up his plate. His big hand, and it was enormously big, caught her wrist and swallowed it, staying her beside him.

"Have you ever touched a man, except to shake hands?" he asked quietly.

"I'm not a shrinking violet," she said, flustered. "I'm almost twenty-two years old, and I have been kissed a few times!"

"Not enough, and not by anyone who knew how." He pulled her closer, feeling her resistance, but he stopped short of dragging her down onto his lap. "Why are you afraid of me?"

"I am not!" she retorted.

His fingers on her wrist were softly caressing. She reacted to him in a way that shocked him. In all the years, with all the women, he'd never felt such response. She was innocent, despite her denials. He'd have bet an oil well on it.

"Calm down," he said softly, feeling so masculine that he could have swallowed a live rattler. He even smiled. "I won't hurt you."

She flushed even more and jerked away from him, but he was much too strong. "Please," she bit off. "Let me go. I don't know how to play this kind of game."

His thumb found her moist palm and rubbed it in a new and exciting way, tracing it softly, causing sensations that went far beyond her hand. "I stopped playing games a long time ago, and I never played them with virgins," he said quietly. "What are you afraid of, Mari?" He spoke her name softly, and she tingled like a schoolgirl.

"You hate women," she said in a voice barely above a whisper. She met his green eyes levelly. "I don't think there's any real feeling in you, any deep emotion. Sometimes you look at me as if you hate me."

He hadn't realized that. He stared down at their hands, hers so pale against his deeply tanned one. "I got burned once, didn't your aunt tell you?"

"I got burned once, too," she replied, "and I don't want to—"

"Again," he finished for her, looking up unexpectedly. "Neither do I."

"Then why don't you let go of my hand?" she asked breathlessly.

He drew it relentlessly to his hard mouth and brushed at it with soft, moist strokes that made her go hot all over. "Why don't you stop me?" he countered. He pried open her palm and touched his tongue to it, and she caught her breath and gasped.

He looked up, his eyes suddenly hotly green and acquisitive, and she felt the first tug of that steely hand on hers with a sense of fantasy. Her eyes were locked into his possessive gaze, her body throbbed with new longings, new curiosities.

"I'm going to teach you a few things you haven't learned," he said, his voice like velvet as he drew her relentlessly down toward him. "And I think it's going to be an explosive lesson for both of us. I feel like a volcano when I touch you..."

Her lips parted as her eyes dropped to his hard, hungry mouth. She could almost see it, feel it, the explosive desire that was going to go up like fireworks when he put his hard mouth on hers and began to touch her.

She almost cried out, the hunger was so formidable. Silence closed in on them. She could hear his breath-

ing, she could feel her heartbeat shaking her. In slow
motion she felt his hard thighs ripple as she was tugged
down onto them, she felt the power and strength of his
hands, smelled the rich fragrance of his cologne, stared
into eyes that wanted her.

She parted her lips in breathless anticipation, aching
for him. Just as his hand went to her shoulder, to draw
her head down, the front door opened with a loud bang.

Chapter Five

Good morning," a pleasant auburn-haired young man was saying before Mari was completely composed again. He seemed to notice nothing, equally oblivious to Mari's flushed face and Ward's uneven breathing.

"Good morning, David," Ward said in what he hoped was a normal voice. From the neck down he had an ache that made speech difficult. "Have some coffee before we start to work."

"No, thank you, sir," the young man said politely. "Actually, I came to ask for a little time off," he added with a sheepish grin. "You see... I've gotten married."

Ward gaped at him. His young secretary had always seemed such a levelheaded boy, with a head full of figures. As it turned out, the figures weren't always the numerical kind.

"Married?" Ward croaked.

"Well, sir, it was kind of a hurried-up thing," David said with a grin. "We eloped. She's such a sweet girl. I was afraid somebody else would snap her up. And I wondered, well, if I could just have a couple of weeks. If you could do without me? If you have to replace me, I'll understand," he added hesitantly.

"Go ahead," Ward muttered. "I'll manage." He shifted in the chair. "What would you like for a wedding present?"

David brightened immediately. "Two weeks off," came the amused reply.

"All right, you've got it. I'll hold your job for the time being. Now get out of here. You know weddings give me indigestion," he added for good measure and then spoiled the whole thing by smiling.

David shook his hand with almost pathetic eagerness. "Thank you, sir!"

"My pleasure. See you in two weeks."

"Yes, sir!" David grinned at Mari, to whom he hadn't even been introduced, and beat a path out the door before he could be called back. He knew his boss pretty well.

"That tears it," Ward grumbled. "What in hell will I do about the mail?"

She stared at him, stunned by his lack of feeling. "He just got married."

"So what?" he demanded. "Surely the only time he really needs to be with her is after dark."

"You male chauvinist!"

"What are you so keyed up about, honey?" he taunted irritably. "Frustrated because I couldn't finish what I started before he walked in on us?"

What good would it do to argue? she asked herself as she noisily loaded up the dirty plates and utensils and took them out to the kitchen without a single word.

He followed her a few minutes later, looking half out of humor and a little guilty.

Standing in the doorway he filled it with his big, tall frame. His hair looked rakish, falling over his broad forehead, and he was so handsome that she had to fight to keep from staring at him all over again.

"I've got to ride over and see about my rig on Tyson Wade's place," he said quietly. "Can you handle the phone?"

"Sure," she told him, walking over to the wall phone. "This is the receiver," she began, pointing to it, speaking in a monotone. "When it rings, you pick it up and talk right in here—"

"Oh, for God's sake," he burst out. "What I meant was that it rings all day long, with everything from stock options to social invitations to notices of board meetings!"

She pushed back her bangs. "I've worked in offices since I was eighteen," she told him.

He cocked his head. "Can you type?"

"How ever do you think I'll manage all the housekeeping and cooking as well as looking after your appointments and answering mail and waiting on Aunt Lillian all at once?" she demanded.

His eyebrows arched. "Well, if you aren't capable of it, I'll hire a cook and a maid and a nurse and a secretary..."

Mari could only imagine how her aunt would react to that. She glared at him. "And break Aunt Lillian's old heart by importing a lot of strangers to keep us apart?"

He laughed in spite of himself. "I guess it would," he confessed. His green eyes narrowed, and there was a light in them that disturbed her as he ran his gaze slowly over her slender body. "God forbid anything should keep us apart."

"Don't you have an oil well to check on?"

"Several, in fact," he agreed. He folded his arms. "But at the moment I'd rather look at you."

"And I'd rather you didn't," she said curtly, averting her eyes to the dishwater.

"I like the way you react to me, Mari," he said softly. "I like the way your body starts to tremble when I come close. If I'd started kissing you a few minute ago, we'd still be doing it. I don't even know if I could stop. And that being the case," he added, leveling with her, "I think you'd better practice ways to discourage me. Lillian won't be around much when she comes back until her leg heals. So you and I are going to get a bit of each other's company. I'd just as soon manage your little visit without showing you how good I am in bed."

His blatant speech shocked her. She turned, soapy hands poised over the sink, and stared at him. "Are you?" she asked without thinking.

He nodded slowly, holding her gaze, his face dead serious. "A man doesn't have to be emotionally involved to make love well. I've had years of practice. But it's never meant much, except physically. It never will. So you keep that in mind, sprout, okay?"

"Okay," she replied, all eyes.

His eyes narrowed at her expression. "Haven't you ever discussed these things with a man?"

"My parents didn't discuss things like that," she replied. "Most of the girls I've known had a distorted view of it because they did it with so many people.

I . . . find the thought of it distasteful, somehow. Sleeping with someone, well, it's intimate, isn't it? Like using someone's toothbrush, only more so. I couldn't . . . just do that, without loving."

She sounded so hopelessly naive. He searched her face and realized with a start that he'd never made love to a virgin. Not one. Not ever. And the thought of touching her in all the ways that he'd touched other women produced a shocking reaction from his body— one he was grateful that she wouldn't recognize.

"What an unusual attitude," he said involuntarily.

"That isn't the word most people use," she replied, her eyes dull and lackluster. "Men avoid me like the plague, except to do typing and answer phones. I'm what's known as an oddball."

"Because you don't sleep around?" he asked, stunned.

"Exactly. Didn't you know that the pill has liberated women?" she explained. "They're allowed the same freedom as men. They can sleep around every night without any consequences. Of course, they sacrifice a few things along the way that the liberals don't mention. Things like that deep-seated guilt that all the permissive ideals in the world won't change."

He stared at her. "My God, you are a fanatic, aren't you?" he mused.

She smiled slowly. "How would you like marrying a woman and hearing all about her old lovers? Meeting them occasionally and wondering if you measured up? How would you like to have a pregnant wife and wonder if the baby was really yours? I mean, if she sleeps around before marriage, what's to keep her from doing it afterward? If promiscuity is okay, isn't adultery okay as well?"

Everything she was saying disturbed him. Caroline had slept around. Not only with him, but, as he'd later found out, with at least two of his business acquaintances. He frowned at the thought. Yes, he'd have wondered. And he'd only just realized it.

"But I'm just a prude," she announced dryly. "So don't mind me. I'll grow into happy spinsterhood and die with the reputation that Elizabeth I had."

"Unless you marry," he said involuntarily.

She laughed ruefully. "Men don't marry women they haven't slept with. Not these days." She turned back to the dishes, oblivious to the brief flash of pain that crossed the face of the man behind her. "I'm not into self-pity, but I do face facts," she continued calmly. "I'm not pretty, I'm just passable. I'm too thin, and I don't know how to flirt. And, as you yourself said, I'm a greenhorn when it comes to intimacy. All that adds up to happy spinsterhood." She gazed thoughtfully out the window over the sink. "I'll grow prize roses," she mused aloud. "Yes, that's what I'll do. And zinnias and crape myrtle and petunias and lantana and hibiscus."

He wasn't listening anymore. He was staring at the back of her head. Her hair was very dark and sleek, and he wished she'd left it long, the way it was in the photograph he'd seen. She wasn't a beauty, that was true. But she had a pretty good sense of humor, and she didn't take herself or anyone else too seriously. She had guts and she told the truth. Damn her.

He didn't like his attraction to her. He didn't like how she could make him tremble all over like a boy when he started to kiss her. He didn't want her knowing it, either. The whole point of this exercise was to *exorcise*. He had to get rid of this lunatic obsession he felt.

"I'm going," he said shortly, shouldering himself away from the doorjamb. "I'll be back by three-thirty to go to the hospital with you."

"I'll phone meanwhile," she said.

"Do what you please." He stormed off, leaving her curious and speechless. What an odd man. What a dangerous man.

She spent the rest of the day working herself into exhaustion so that she wouldn't dwell on what had happened at breakfast.

When they got to the hospital, Lillian was sitting on the side of her bed, dressed.

"It's about time," she began hotly. "Get me out of here! They've put on a cast and decided it was infected sinuses that made me fall. They've given me some tablets they say will lower my blood pressure, and if you don't spring me, I'll jump out a window!"

"With that?" Ward asked, nodding toward the heavy plaster walking cast on one of her legs.

"With that," she assured him. "Tell him I'm serious about this, Mari," she added.

Mari was trying not to laugh. "You look pretty serious."

"I can see that. Where's the doctor?"

"He'll be here any minute," Lillian began.

"I'll go find him," Ward returned, walking quickly out into the hall, moving lightly for a man his size.

"How's it going?" Lillian asked, all eyes.

"How's what going?" Mari asked with assumed innocence.

"You were alone all last night!" she hissed. "Did he try anything?"

Mari lifted her eyebrows and pursed her lips. ''Well, he did try to call somebody on the phone, but he couldn't get them.''

Lillian looked pained. ''I mean, did he make a pass at you?''

''No,'' Mari lied. It was only a white lie, just enough to throw the bloodhound off the scent.

The older woman looked miserable. It didn't bode well that Ward was so irritable, either. Maybe her matched pair had been arguing. Lillian had to get out of here and do a little stage-managing before it was too late and her whole plan went down the tube!

Ward was back minutes later, looking as unapproachable as he had since he'd driven up to the house at three-thirty with a face like a thunderhead.

''I found him. He says you're okay, no stroke,'' he told Lillian. ''You can leave. I've signed you out. Let's go.''

''But we need a wheelchair...'' Mari began.

He handed her Lillian's purse, lifted the elderly woman easily in his arms and carried her out the door, his set features daring anyone to question or stop him.

Back at Three Forks Lillian's room was on the ground floor, and despite all the protests she immediately returned to the kitchen and started supper.

''Do you want to go back to the hospital?'' Ward demanded, hands on hips, glaring. ''Get into bed!''

''I can cook with a broken leg,'' she returned hotly. ''It isn't my hands that don't work, and I've never yet used my toes!''

He sighed angrily. ''Mari can do that.''

''Mari's answering your letters,'' he was pointedly reminded. ''She can't do everything. And with David gone...''

"Damn David," he muttered darkly. "What a hell of a time to get married!"

Lillian glared at him until he muttered something rough under his breath and strode off toward his den.

Mari was inside the paneled room, working away at the computer. She was trying to erase a mistake and was going crazy deciphering the language of the computer he'd shown her. The word processing program was one of the most expensive and the most complicated. She couldn't even get it to backspace.

"I can't do anything with your aunt," he grumbled, slamming the door. "She's sitting on a stool making a pie."

"No wonder you can't do anything with her," she commented innocently. "Your stomach won't let you."

He glared at her. "How's it going?"

She sighed. "Don't you have a typewriter?"

"What year do you think this is?" he demanded. "What kind of equipment have you got at that garage where you work?"

"A manual typewriter," she said.

His head bent forward. "A what?"

"A manual type—"

"That's what I thought you said. My God!"

"Well, until they hired me, one of the men was doing all the office work. They thought the manual typewriter was the latest thing. It did beat handwriting all the work orders," she added sweetly.

"I work with modern equipment," he told her, gesturing toward the computer. "That's faster than even an electronic typewriter, and you can save what you do. I thought you knew how to use it."

"I know how to turn it on," she agreed brightly.

He moved behind her and peered over her shoulder. "Is that all you've done so far?"

"I've only been in here an hour," she reminded him. "It took me that long to discover what to stuff into the big slots."

"Diskettes," he said. "Program diskettes."

"Whatever. Anyway, this manual explains how to build a nuclear device, not how to use the word processing program," she said, pushing the booklet away. "Or it might as well. I don't understand a word of it. Could you show me how it works?" She looked up at him with eyes the color of a robin's egg.

He actually forgot what he was saying. She had a way of looking at him that made his blood thaw, like the sun beating down on an icy pond. He could imagine how a colt felt on a spring morning with the breeze stirring and juicy grass to eat and a big pasture to run in.

"Could you?" she prompted, lost in his green eyes.

His big hand touched the side of her face tentatively, his thumb moving over her mouth, exploring its soft texture, mussing her lipstick, sensitizing her lips until they parted on a caught breath.

"Could I what, Mari?" he asked in a tone that curled her toes inside her shoes.

Her head was much too far back. It gave him access to her mouth. She saw the intent in his narrowing eyes, in his taut stance. Her body ached for his touch. She looked up at him helplessly, his willing victim, wanting his mouth on hers with a passion that overwhelmed her.

He bent slowly, letting his gaze fall to her parted lips. She could smell the heady fragrance of his cologne now because he was so close. There was mint and coffee on his breath, and he had strong white teeth; she could see them where his chiseled lips parted in anticipation of possession. Her breasts throbbed, and she noticed a tingling, yearning sensation there.

"Your skin is hot," he whispered, tracing her cheek with his fingers as he tilted his face across hers and moved even closer. "I can feel it burning."

Her hands were on his arms now. She could feel the powerful muscles through the white shirt that he'd worn with a tie and jacket when they went to pick up Lillian. But the jacket and tie were gone, and the shirt was partially unbuttoned, and now the overwhelming sight of him filled Mari's world. Her short nails pressed into his skin, bending against those hard muscles as his lips brushed over hers.

"Bite me," he whispered huskily and then incited her to do it, teasing her mouth, teaching her.

She knew nothing, but she wanted so desperately to please him so that he wouldn't stop. This was magic, and she wanted more.

Her mouth opened and she nipped at his firm lower lip, nibbling it, feeling its softness. He laughed softly deep in his throat, and she felt his hand move from her cheek to her shoulder, down her arm to her waist. While he played with her mouth, his fingers splayed out and then moved up, and the thin fabric of her flowery shirtwaist dress was no barrier at all as he found her rib cage and began to tease it.

This was explosive. Mari trembled a little because she was catching fire. He hadn't been kidding when he told her he was a good lover. She hadn't dreamed of the kind of sensations that he was showing her. She hadn't realized how vulnerable she was. Her mind was telling her that it was a game, that he didn't mean it. He'd said so. But her body was enthralled by new feelings, new pleasures, and it wouldn't let her stop.

"Oh," she whispered unsteadily when his tongue began to taste the soft inner surface of her lips.

"Open my shirt," he whispered against her warm mouth. He drew her hands to the remaining buttons and coaxed them until they had the fabric away from him.

She put her hands against hard muscle and thick hair and gasped at the contact. She'd never touched a man this way, and he knew it and was excited by it.

He bit her lower lip with a slow, ardent pressure that was arousing. "Draw your nails down to my belt," he murmured against her parted mouth.

She did, amazed at the shudder of his big body, at the soft groan her caress produced. She drew away slightly so that she could see his face, could see the lazy, smoldering desire in his green eyes.

"I like it," he told her with a husky laugh.

She did it again, lowering her eyes this time to watch his muscles ripple with pleasure as she stroked them, to watch his flat stomach draw in even more with a caught breath. It was exciting to arouse him. It gave her a sense of her femininity that she'd never experienced.

Meanwhile, his hand was moving again, this time up her rib cage. Not blatant but subtle in its caress, teasing lightly, provocative. It reached the outer edges of her breast even as her nails were tenderly scoring him, and his fingers lifted to touch around her nipple.

She shuddered, looking up at him with the residue of virginal fear in her wide blue eyes. Her hand went to his hairy wrist and poised there while she tried to choose between pleasure and guilt.

"Have you ever done this before?" he asked, his lips against hers.

"No," she confessed.

Odd, how protective that made him feel. And how much a man. He brushed his lips gently over hers. "Lillian isn't fifty feet away," he whispered. "And we won't do anything horribly indiscreet. But I'm as excited by this as you are, and I don't want to stop just yet. I want to touch you and feel your reaction and let you feel mine. Mari," he murmured, tracing a path up her soft breast, "I've never been the first. Not in any way, even this. Let me teach you. I promise you, there's not the slightest danger. Not right now."

"Oh, but I shouldn't..." She was weakening and her voice betrayed her.

"Don't feel guilty," he whispered over her mouth. "This is love play. Women and men have indulged themselves this way since the beginning of time. I'm human. So are you. There's no shame in being hungry."

He made it sound natural. It was the seducer's basic weapon, but Mari was too outmatched to care. She arched toward his fingers because she couldn't help herself. That maddening tracing of his fingers was driving her to her limits. She wanted his hand to flatten on her body. She wanted him to touch her... there!

His teeth nibbled at her lower lip, catching it in a soft tug just as his fingers closed on an erect nipple and tightened gently.

She cried out. The sound would have penetrated the walls and door, but he caught it in his mouth and muffled it, half mad with unexpected arousal. Her cries and her trembling were driving him over the edge.

Somehow he had her on the sofa, flat on her back with his heavy body half covering her. Her dress was coming undone, she could feel the air on her bare skin, and her bra was all too loose, and his hand was...there.

She shuddered and her eyes opened, hazy with passion. Her mouth was swollen, her cheeks red, her upward gaze full of rapt wonder.

His big hand flattened over her soft breast, feeling the tip rub abrasively on his palm as he caressed her. His thumb circled it roughly, and she shuddered all over, her breath sighing out unsteadily like his own.

She wanted him to kiss her some more, but his eyes were on her dress now. He peeled it slowly away from the breast he was touching, moving her bra up so that he could see the pink and mauve contrast and that taut little nub. It was as if he'd never looked at a woman before. She was beautiful. Sweetly curving and high, and not too big or too little. Just right.

She felt as if she were watching from a distance. Her eyes wandered over his absorbed expression, seeing the veiled pleasure there, the wonder. If she was awed by him, so was he awed by her. He was touching her like some priceless treasure, taking his time, lovingly tracing every texture.

He took the nipple between his thumb and forefinger and felt its hardness. He looked up into her fascinated eyes. "If I put my mouth on you, you'll cry out again," he whispered softly. "And Lillian might mistake the sound and come hopping."

She was trembling. She wanted it. Her body arched sinuously. She reached up, shyly, and cupped his face, gently tugging at it.

"I won't...cry out," she whispered, biting her lower lip to make sure.

"Say 'taste me,'" he whispered back, searching her eyes.

She blushed feverishly and turned her face into his throat to hide her embarrassment.

"Virgin," he breathed, trembling himself with the newness of it. "Oh, God, I want to have you so much!"

She thought she knew what he meant, but just then he took her breast into his warm mouth, and she had to chew her lip almost through to keep from screaming at the incredible sensation.

Her hands released his face, and she clenched them over her head. Writhing helplessly, she was caught up in the throes of something so powerful that it stopped her breath in her throat. She twisted up toward him, her body shuddering, her breast on fire with the feel of his mouth.

With a rough groan he suddenly rolled away from her and sat up with his face in his hands, shuddering, bent over as if in agony.

She lay there without moving, shaking all over with reaction and frustration, too weak from desire to even cover herself.

After a minute he took a deep, steadying breath and looked down at her. If she expected mockery or amusement, she was surprised. Because he wasn't smiling.

His dark green eyes ran over her like hands, lingering on all the places where his mouth had been, devouring her. He drew the bra slowly back down and reached around her for the hooks, fastening them. Then he pulled the edges of her dress together and buttoned them. He didn't speak until he was through.

"Do you understand why I stopped?" he asked gently. Yes, there was that. There was tenderness in every line of his face, in his voice, in the fingers that brushed her cheek.

"Yes," she returned slowly. "I think so."

"I didn't frighten you?"

That seemed to matter very much. She felt suddenly old and venerable and deeply possessive. "No," she said.

He tugged gently on a strand of damp hair. "Did I please you?" he persisted and this time he smiled but without mockery.

"As if you couldn't tell," she murmured, lowering her face so that he couldn't see it.

"If we ever make love completely, it will have to be in a soundproof room," he said at her ear. "You'd scream the house down."

"Ward!" she groaned and buried her face in his chest.

"No." He shuddered, moving her away, and he looked pale all of a sudden.

Her eyes questioned his. All these feeling were very new to her.

He drew in a harsh breath, holding her hands in his. "Men are very easy to arouse," he told her without embarrassment. "When they get to fever pitch, it takes very little to fan the fire. Right now I'm beyond fever pitch," he mused with a faint laugh, "and if you touch me that way again, we're both going to be in a lot of trouble."

"Oh," she returned, searching his eyes. "Does it hurt?" she whispered softly.

"A little," he replied. He brushed back her hair. "How about you?"

"Wow." She laughed shakily. "I never dreamed that could happen to me."

He felt incredible. New. Reborn. He touched her face lightly as if he were dreaming. Bending over her, he took her mouth softly under his and kissed her. It was different from any other kiss in his life. When he let her go, he had to stand up or lay her down.

"You'd better get back to work," he said and gestured toward the computer. "And, no, I'm not going to try to teach you. My body won't let me that close without making impossible demands on both of us so you'll have to muddle through alone." He laughed angrily. "Damn it, are you a witch?"

She stood up, smoothing her dress and hair. "Actually, until about five minutes ago, I thought I was Lady Dracula."

"Now you know better, don't you?" He stood watching her, his mouth slightly swollen, his shirt open, his hands on his narrow hips. The sight of him still took her breath away.

She went quickly back to the computer and sat down, keeping her eyes on the screen. "I'll get these finished before supper, if I can," she promised.

He smiled to himself. It took him a minute to leave her, his mind grappling furiously with the conflict between his desire and his calculating mind that insisted she was only interested in what he had—his ranch, his oil, his money.

Women had never wanted him for himself; why should Mari be different? But why had she reacted with such sweet ardor unless she'd wanted him as desperately as he'd wanted her? That kind of fever was hard to fake. No, he thought. No, she'd wanted him. But was she really that unmaterialistic? The only women he'd let himself get close to were his mother and Caroline, both of whom had been self-centered opportunists. How could he trust this one? She bothered him terribly. He no longer felt any confidence in his own judgment. He left the room scowling.

Chapter Six

Mari was so shaken by what had happened with Ward that she had eventually needed to escape from the den. She was afraid everything they'd done would show on her face, and Lillian had sharp eyes. She also wondered if Ward would tease her. That would be the last straw, to have a worldly man like that make fun of her for a physical reaction she couldn't help.

She needn't have worried. Ward was nowhere in sight, and Lillian was muttering furiously as she hobbled around the kitchen with a crutch under one arm.

"I wish you'd let me do that," Mari scolded. She picked up the plate of ham that Lillian was trying to take to the table and carried it in for her. "You shouldn't be trying to lift things, Aunt Lillian. You know what the doctor said."

"Yes, but it's pretty hard asking people for help," the older woman said irritably. She glanced at Mari. "He's gone."

Mari tried to look innocent. "He?"

"The boss. He decided to fly down to South America. Just like that." She snapped her fingers while Mari tried not to let her eyes reflect the shock she felt.

"He left tonight?" Mari asked blankly. It didn't seem possible. She'd been talking with him—among other things—less than two hours ago.

"Yep. He sure did. Bag and baggage. Imagine, getting a flight out of here that quickly. He'll go on a commercial flight from San Antonio, you see." She added, "Flew himself over to the airport, he did."

Mari cleared her throat. "You said a few days ago that he'd have to go to South America."

"Yes. But I didn't expect him to leave in the middle of my first night back home," Lillian said hotly.

"He knows I'm here," she returned and impulsively hugged the older woman. "I'll take care of you."

Lillian sighed miserably. "Nothing is working the way it was meant to," she grumbled. "Nothing!"

Now was her chance to perfect her acting ability. "Whatever do you mean, Aunt Lillian?" she asked with a smile.

Lillian actually flushed. "Nothing. Not a thing. Here, set the table and help me get the food in here. There'll be a lot for just the two of us, seeing the boss and his appetite are missing, but we can freeze the rest, I suppose."

"Did you take your pill?" Mari asked.

Lillian glowered at her. Then she grinned. "Yep."

"Good for you," Mari returned. "Now I'll get to keep you for a lot longer."

Lillian started to speak, and then she just laughed. But her eyes were troubled when she hobbled back out to the kitchen.

* * *

Mari wandered around by herself during the next few days, when she wasn't helping Lillian, enjoying the spaciousness of the ranch and the feeling of being self-sufficient. It must have been very much like this a hundred years before, she thought as she gazed out at the level horizon, when bad men and cattlemen and refugees from the Confederacy had come through on the long trails that led north and south and west.

It was so quiet. Nothing like the noisy bustle of Atlanta. Mari felt at peace here, she felt safe. But she missed Ward in ways that she never would have expected. She'd only really known him for a matter of days, but even that made no difference to her confused emotions. She could close her eyes and feel his hard mouth, his hands holding her, touching her. It had been the most exquisite thing that she'd ever experienced, being in his arms that day. She wanted it again, so much.

But even wanting it, she realized how dangerous it was to let him that close a second time. He only wanted her, he'd admitted that. He didn't believe in marriage. Apparently, he'd had a rough time with a woman at some point in his life, and he'd been soured. Aunt Lillian had mentioned that his mother ran away with another man, leaving Ward and Belinda to be raised by their grandmother. So she couldn't really blame him for his attitude. But that didn't make her own emotions any easier to handle.

She found herself watching the driveway and looking out the window, waiting. When the phone rang, and it did constantly, she ran to answer it, sure that it would be him. But it never was. Five days passed, and despite the fact that she enjoyed Aunt Lillian's company, she was restless. It was almost the end of her vacation. She'd have to leave. What if she never saw him again before she had to go?

"Missing the boss?" Lillian asked one evening, eyeing her niece calculatingly over the chicken and stuffing the younger woman wasn't touching.

Mari actually jumped. "No. Of course not."

"Not even a little?"

Mari sighed as she toyed with a fresh roll. "Maybe a little."

Lillian smiled. "That's nice. Because he's just coming up the driveway."

Mari couldn't stop herself. She leaped up from the table and ran to the front door, threw it open and darted out onto the porch. She caught herself just before she dashed down the steps toward him. She hadn't realized until that moment just how deeply involved she already was. Boys had never paid her much attention. Surely it was just the newness of being touched and kissed. Wasn't it?

She held on to the porch railing, forcing herself not to take one more step.

He got out of the Chrysler, looking as out of humor as when he'd left, a flight bag slung over one shoulder. Striking in a deep-tan vested suit and creamy Stetson, he closed the door with a hard slam, turned and started for the steps. Then he spotted Mari and stood quite still, just looking.

She was wearing a gauzy sea-green blouse with beige slacks, and she looked young and very pretty and a little lonely. His heart shot up into his throat, and all the bad temper seeped out.

"Well, hello, little lady," he said, moving up the steps, and he was actually smiling.

"Hello." She forced herself to look calm. "Did you have a good trip?"

"I guess so."

He stopped just in front of her, and she could see new lines in his face, dark circles under his eyes. Had he been with some woman? Her eyes narrowed curiously.

"Do I look that bad?" he taunted.

"You look tired," she murmured.

"I am. I did two weeks' business in five days." He searched her big, soft blue eyes quietly. "Miss me?"

"I had lots to do," she hedged. "And the phone hasn't stopped."

"That's not surprising." He let the bag fall to the porch and took her face in his big hands, tilting it up to his curious green eyes. "Dark circles," he murmured, running his thumbs gently under her eyes. "You haven't slept, have you?"

"You look like you haven't, either," she returned. There was a note in her voice that surprised and secretly delighted him.

"I never mix business with women," he whispered lazily. "It's bad policy. I haven't been sleeping around with any of those gorgeous, dark-eyed Latins."

"Oh." She felt embarrassed and lowered her shocked eyes to his chest. "That's none of my business, after all," she began.

"Wouldn't you like it to be?" he asked softly. He leaned toward her, nuzzling her face so that she lifted it helplessly and met his quiet, steady gaze. "Or would you rather pretend that what we did the night I left meant nothing at all to you?"

"It meant nothing at all to you," she countered. "You even said so, that you . . ."

He stopped the soft tirade with his mouth. His arm reached across her back, pillowing her head, and his free hand spread on her throat, smoothing its silky softness as he ravished the warm sweetness of her parted lips. He was hungry, and he didn't lift his head for a long time, not until he felt her begin to tremble, not until he heard the soft gasp and felt the eager ardor of her young mouth.

He was breathing through his nose, heavily, and his eyes frightened her a little. "You haunted me, damn you," he said roughly, spearing his fingers into her thick dark hair. "In my sleep I heard you cry out..."

"Don't hurt me," she whispered shakily, her eyes pleading with him. "I'm not experienced enough, I'm not...old enough...to play adult games with men."

That stopped him, softened him. The harsh light went out of his eyes, and he searched her delicate features with growing protectiveness.

"I'll never hurt you," he whispered and meant it. He kissed her eyes closed. "Not that way or in bed. Oh, God, Mari, you make me ache like a teenager!"

Her nails bit into his arms as he started to lean toward her again, and just as his lips touched hers in the prelude to what would have become a violently passionate exchange, they heard the soft, heavy thud of Lillian's cast as she headed toward them.

"Cupid approaches," he muttered, a subtle tremor in the hands that gently put her away from him. "She'd die if she knew what she just interrupted."

Mari stared at him, a little frightened by her lack of resistance, by the blatant hunger that she'd felt.

"Passion shouldn't be frightening to you," he said gently as the thuds grew closer. "It's as natural as breathing."

She shifted, watching him lift his bag without moving his eyes from her. "It's very new," she whispered.

"Then it's new for both of us," he said just before Lillian opened the door. "Because I've never felt this with another woman. And if that shocks you, it should. It damned well shocks me. I thought I'd done it all."

"Welcome home, boss." Lillian beamed, holding the door back. "You look good. Doesn't he, Mari?" Flushed face on the girl, and the boss looked a little flustered. Good. Good. Things were progressing. Absence worked after all.

"I feel pretty good, too," he returned, putting an affectionate arm around Lillian. "Been behaving?"

"Yes, sir. Pills and all." Lillian glared at her niece. "It's pretty hard not to take pills when you're threatened with being rolled in a towel."

He laughed warmly, glancing over at Mari. "Good girl."

"I should get medals for this," Mari returned, her eyes searching his, searching his face, quiet and curious and puzzled.

He hugged Lillian. "No doubt. What's for dinner? I'm starved."

"Finally," Lillian said with a grin. "Things are back to normal. You should see all the food I've saved up."

"Don't just stand there, both of you, go fetch it," he said, looking starved. "I'll die if I don't eat soon!"

Lillian responded to his order, producing an abundance of hearty food. While Ward dug in, Mari watched him with pure admiration. She'd never seen a human being put it away with such pleasure. He didn't seem to gain an ounce, for all his appetite. But then he was on the run most of his life, which probably explained his trim but masculine build.

He finished the last of the dressing and sat back with a heavy sigh to sip his second cup of coffee while Lillian, despite offers of help and threats, pushed a trolley of dirty dishes out to the kitchen and dishwasher.

"She won't slow down," Mari said. "I've tried, but she won't let me take over. I called the doctor, but he said as long as she was taking her medicine and didn't overdo standing on that cast, she'd be okay. I do at least get her to sit down, and I help when she lets me."

"Good thing her room's on the ground floor," he remarked.

"Yes."

He studied her over the rim of his coffee cup, his eyes narrow and quiet and full of green flames. There was no amusement in them now, no mockery. Just frank, blatant desire.

She looked back because it was beyond her powers of resistance not to. He held her in thrall, his darkening eyes full of promised pleasure, exquisite physical delight. Her body recognized that look, even if her brain didn't, and began to respond in frightening ways.

"I should bring in the dessert," she said as she rose, panicked.

"I don't want dessert," he said deeply.

She thought she knew what he did want, and she almost said so, but she dropped back down into her chair and put more sugar in her already oversweet coffee.

"Keep that up, and you can take rust off with it." He nodded toward her efforts with the sugar bowl.

She flushed. "I like it sweet."

"Do you?" He reached over and stilled her hand, his fingers lightly caressing it. While he held her eyes, he took the spoon away from her and linked his fingers slowly with hers in a light, caressing pressure that made her want to scream with frustrated hunger.

She couldn't help it. Her fingers contracted, too, convulsively, and she looked at him with aching desire.

His face went hard. "Suppose we go over those phone messages?" he asked.

"All right."

They both knew it was only an excuse, a reason to be alone together in the den to make love. Because that was surely what was going to happen. Being apart and then experiencing this explosive togetherness had taken its toll on them. He stood up and drew her along with him, and she could feel the throbbing silence that grew as they walked down the hall.

"Don't you want dessert?" Lillian called after them but not very heartily. She was grinning too much.

"Not right now," Ward replied. He looked down at Mari as he opened the door to the den, and there were blazing fires in his steady, possessive eyes.

Mari felt her lips part as she looked up at him. She started past him, feeling the warmth of his big body, the strength and power of it, and smelling his spicy cologne. She could hardly wait to be alone with him.

Just as he started to follow her into the room, into the secret silence of it, the heady atmosphere was shattered by a loud knock at the front door.

He cursed under his breath, whirling with such unexpected violence that Mari felt sorry for whoever was out there.

He opened the door and glared out. "Well?" he demanded.

"Well, you invited me, didn't you?" came an equally curt reply in a voice as deep and authoritative as Ward's. "You called me from the airport and said come

over and we'd work out that second lease. So here I am.
Or did you forget?''

"No."

"Do you want to serve my coffee on the damned
porch?"

Ward tried not to grin, but he couldn't help it. Honest to God, Ty Wade was just like him.

"Oh, hell, come in," he muttered, holding the door
open.

A tall, whipcord-lean man entered the house, Stetson in hand. He was as homely as leftover bacon, and
he had eyes so piercing and coldly gray that Mari almost backed away. And then he saw her and smiled,
and his face changed.

"Marianne, this is my neighbor, Tyson Wade," Ward
told her curtly.

Ty nodded without speaking, glancing past Mari to
where Lillian was standing in her cast. "What did you
do, kick him?" he asked Lillian, nodding toward Ward.

Lillian laughed. "Not quite. How are Erin and the
twins?"

"Just beautiful, thanks," Ty said with a quiet smile.

"Give them my best," Lillian said. "Coffee?"

"Just make it, I'll come and get the tray," Ward said
firmly.

Lillian grumbled off toward the kitchen while Mari
searched for words.

"I think I'll turn in," she said to Ward. "If you still
want me to help with the office work, I need to get some
sleep so that I can start early."

Ward looked harder than usual. Mari couldn't know
that seeing Ty and the change marriage had made in
him had knocked every amorous thought right out of
his head. Ty spelled commitment, and Ward wanted

none of it. So why in hell, he was asking himself, had he been coming on to a virgin?

"Sure," he told Mari. "You do that. If you don't mind, try to get your aunt into bed, too, could you? She's going to make a basket case of me if she doesn't start resting. Tell her that, too. Play on her conscience, girl."

Mari forced a smile. "I'll try. Nice to meet you, Mr. Wade," she told Ty and went after Lillian.

"Imagine, Tyson Wade in this very house," Lillian said with a sigh as she fixed a tray. "It's been a shock, seeing those two actually talk. They've been feuding as long as I've worked here. Then Mr. Wade got married and just look at him."

"He seems very much a family man," Mari commented.

"You should have seen him before." Lillian grinned. "He made the boss look like a pussycat."

"That bad?"

"That bad. Bad enough, in fact, to make the boss get rid of a half-wolf, half-shepherd dog he loved to death. It brought down some of Ty's cattle, and he came over here to 'discuss it' with the boss." She turned, grinning at her niece. "The very next day that dog was adopted into a good home. And the boss had to see his dentist. Tyson Wade was a mean man before Miss Erin came along. Ah, the wonder of true love." She gave Mari a sizing-up look and grinned even more when the younger woman blushed. "Well, let's get to the dishes, if you're determined to get in my way."

Mari was and she did, quickly shooing Lillian out. Then she disappeared herself before Ward came for the coffee tray. She'd had enough for one night.

* * *

Breakfast was an ordeal, Ward was cold all of a sudden, not the amorous, very interested man of the day before. Mari felt cold and empty and wondered what she'd done to make him look at her with those indifferent eyes. She was beginning to be glad that her vacation was almost over.

He followed her into the office and started opening mail. It had piled up in his absence, and he frowned over the amount waiting for him.

"Can you take dictation?" he asked Mari without looking up.

"Yes."

"Okay. Get a pad and pen out of the desk drawer and let's get started."

He began to dictate. The first letter was in response to a man who owed Ward money. The man had written Ward to explain that he'd had a bad month and would catch up on his payments as soon as he could. Instead of an understanding reply, Ward dictated a scorching demand for full payment that ended in a threatened lawsuit.

Mari started to speak, but the look he gave her was an ultimatum. She forced back the words and kept her silence.

Each letter was terse, precise and without the least bit of compassion. She began to get a picture of him that was disappointing and disillusioning. If there was any warmth in him, she couldn't find it in business. Perhaps that was why he was so wealthy. He put his own success above the problems of his creditors. So he had money. And apparently not much conscience. But Mari had one, and the side of him that she was seeing disturbed her greatly.

Finally Ward was finished dictating the letters, but just as she started to type them, the phone rang. Ward answered it, his face growing darker with every instant.

It was a competitor on the phone, accusing him of using underhanded methods to get the best of a business deal. He responded with language that should have caused the telephone company to remove his phone and burn it. Mari was the color of a boiled lobster when he finished and hung up.

"Something bothering you, honey?" he chided.

"You're ruthless," she said quietly.

"Hell, yes, I am," he returned without embarrassment. "I grew up the butt of every cruel tongue in town. I was that Jessup boy, the one whose mother was the easiest woman around and ran off with Mrs. Hurdy's husband. I was that poor kid down the road that never had a decent family except for his battle-ax of a grandmother." His green eyes glowed, and she wondered if he'd ever said these things to anyone else. "Success is a great equalizer, didn't you know? The same people who used to look down their noses at me now take off their hats and nod these days. I'm on everybody's guest list. I get recognized by local civic groups. I'm always being mentioned in the newspapers. Oh, I'm a big man these days, sprout." His face hardened. "But I wasn't always. Not until I had money. And how I get it doesn't bother me. Why should I be a good old boy in business? Nobody else is."

"Isn't Mr. Wade?" she fished.

"Mr. Wade," he informed her, "is now a family man, and he's missing his guts. His wife removed them, along with his manhood and his pride."

She stood. "What a terrible thing to say," she burst out. "How can you be so coldhearted? Don't you realize what you're doing to yourself? You're shriveling up into an old Scrooge, and you don't seem to realize it."

"I give to charity," he said arrogantly.

"For appearances and to get ahead," she replied hotly. "Not because you care. You don't, do you? You don't really care about one living soul."

His chin lifted and his eyes sparkled dangerously. "I care about my grandmother and my sister. And maybe Lillian."

"And nobody else," she said, hurt a bit by his admission that he didn't feel a thing for her.

"That's right," he said coldly. "Nobody else."

She stood there with her hands clenched at her sides, hurting in ways that she'd never expected she could. "You're a real prince, aren't you?" she asked.

"I'm a rich one, too," he returned, smiling slowly. "But if you had any ideas about taking advantage of that fact, you can forget them. I like my money's worth. And I'm not suited to wedding cake and rice."

When what he had said finally broke through the fog and she realized what he was accusing her of, she had to bite her tongue to keep from crying. So that was what he thought—that she was nothing but a gold digger, out to set herself up for life on his fortune.

"I know," she said with an icy look. "And that's good because most women who are looking for a husband want one who doesn't have to be plugged into a wall socket to warm up!"

"Get out of my office," he said shortly. "Since you're here to visit your aunt, go do it and keep the hell out of my way! When I want a sermon, I'll get it in church!"

"Any minister who got you into church would be canonized!" she told him bluntly and ran out of the room.

She didn't tell Lillian what had happened. Shortly thereafter Ward stormed out, slamming the door behind him. He didn't come back until well after bedtime. Mari hadn't gone back into the den, and by the time she crawled into bed, she was already planning how to tell Aunt Lillian that she'd have to return to Georgia.

It wouldn't be easy to leave. But now that she'd had a glimpse of the real man, the character under the veneer, she was sure that she was doing the right thing. Ward Jessup might be a rich man with a fat wallet. But he was ice-cold. If she had any sanity left, she'd get away from him before her addiction got so bad that she'd find excuses to stay just to look at him.

That remark about not caring for anyone except family had hurt terribly. She did understand why he was the way he was, but it didn't help her broken heart. She'd been learning to love him. And now she found that he had nothing at all to give. Not even warmth. It was the worst blow of all. Yes, she'd have to go home now. Aunt Lillian was coping beautifully, taking her medicine and even resting properly. At least Ward would take care of the older woman. He cared about *her*. He'd never care about Mari, and it was high time she faced facts.

Chapter Seven

Mari had a miserable day. She kept out of Ward's way, and she didn't go back into the den. Let him get a temporary secretary, she thought furiously, if he couldn't manage his dirty work alone. She wasn't going to do it for him.

"Talk about unarmed conflict," Lillian muttered as Mari went out the back door in a lightweight jacket and jeans.

"He started it," Mari said irritably. "Or didn't you know how he did business?"

Lillian's expression said that she did. "He's a hard man to understand sometimes," she said, her voice gentle, coaxing. "But you can't imagine the life he's had, Mari. People aren't cold without reason. Very often it's just a disguise."

"His is flawless."

"So is yours," Lillian said with a warm smile. "Almost. But don't give up on him yet. He might surprise you."

"He won't have time. Have you forgotten that I have to go home in two more days?"

The older woman looked worried. "Yes, I know. I had hoped you might stay a little longer."

"You're feeling better," she returned. "And he doesn't want me here. Not anymore. I'm not even sure I'd stay if I was asked." She opened the door. "I'm going to look at the horses."

She walked out without another word, crestfallen and miserable. She stuck her hands in the pockets of her jacket and walked aimlessly along the fence until she came in sight of the barn.

There he was, sitting astride a huge chestnut-colored horse, his working clothes making him look even bigger than usual, his Stetson cocked over one eye. Watching her.

She stopped in her tracks, glaring at him. He urged the horse into a slow trot and reined in beside her, resting his crossed hands on the pommel. The leather creaked as he shifted in the saddle and pushed back his hat.

"Are we still speaking?" he asked, his tone half amused.

"Can someone run me to the bus station in the morning?" she asked, ignoring the question. "My vacation is up the day after tomorrow. I have to get back to Atlanta."

He stared at her for a long moment before he spoke. "How are you going to explain that decision to Lillian?" he asked, carefully choosing his words. "You're supposed to think I'm dying, aren't you? You're supposed to be helping me write my memoirs.''

"I don't think my stomach is strong enough," she replied.

His green eyes glittered at her. "Stop that. I'm trying to make friends with you."

"I tried to make friends with a gerbil once," she commented. "I stuck my hand down into its cage to let it have a nice sniff, and it tried to eat my little finger."

"You're making this difficult," he grumbled, tilting his hat back over his eyes.

"No, you are," she corrected. "I'm doing my best to relieve you of my gold-digging, sermonizing presence."

He sighed heavily, searching her eyes. "I've never had to justify myself to anyone," he told her. "I've never wanted to." He studied the pommel as if he hadn't seen one before, examining it as he spoke. "I don't want you to go, Mari."

Her heart ran away. "Why not?"

He shrugged and smiled faintly. "Maybe I've gotten used to you." He looked up. "Besides, your aunt will never get over it if you leave right now. All her plans for us will be ruined."

"That's a foregone conclusion as far as I'm concerned," she said, her voice curt. She clenched her hands in her pockets. "I wouldn't have you on a stick, roasted."

He had to work to keep from grinning. "Wouldn't you?"

"I'm going home," she repeated.

He tilted his hat back again. "You don't have a job."

"I do so. I work at a garage!"

"Not anymore." He did grin this time. "I called them last week and told them that you had to quit to take care of your sick aunt and her 'dying' employer."

"You what!"

"It seemed like the thing to do at the time," he said conversationally. "They said they were real sorry, and it sure was lucky they'd just had a girl apply for a job that morning. I'll bet they hired her that very day."

She could hardly breathe through her fury. She felt as if her lungs were on fire. "You...you...!" She searched for some names she'd heard at the garage and began slinging them at him.

"Now, shame on you," he scolded, bending unexpectedly to drag her up to sit in the saddle in front of him. "Sit still!" he said roughly, controlling the excited horse with one hand on the reins while the other was on Mari.

"I hate you," she snapped.

He got the gelding under control and wheeled it, careful not to jerk the reins and unseat them both. The high-strung animal took gentle handling. "Care to prove that?" he asked.

She didn't ask what he meant. There was no time. She was too busy trying to hold on to the pommel. She hadn't realized how far off the ground that saddle was until she was sitting in it. Behind her, she felt the warm strength of his powerful body, and if she hadn't been so nervous, she might have felt the tense set of it in the saddle.

He rode into a small grove of oak and mesquite trees and dismounted. Before she knew it, she was out of the saddle and flat on her back in the lush spring grass with Ward's hard face above her.

"Now," he said gently, "suppose you show me how much you hate me?"

His dark head bent, and she reached up, unthinking, to catch his thick hair and push him away. But it only gave him an unexpected opening, and she caught her breath as his full weight came down over her body, crushing her into the leaves and grass.

"Better give in, honey, or you could sink down all the way to China," he commented wickedly. His hands were resting beside her head, and somehow he'd caught hers in them. He had her effectively pinned, without any effort at all, and was just short of gloating about it. He wasn't trying to spare her his formidable weight, either, and she could just barely breathe.

She panted, struggling, until she felt what her struggles were accomplishing and reluctantly subsided. She contented herself with glaring up at him from a face the color of pickled beets.

"Coward," he chided.

She was very still, barely breathing. His hands were squeezing hers, but with a caressing pressure not a brutal one. The look in his eyes was slowly changing from faint amusement to dark passion. If she hadn't recognized the look, his body would have told her as he began to move subtly over hers, sensually, with a practiced expertness that even her innocence recognized.

"Yes, that makes you tremble, doesn't it?" he breathed, watching her as his hips caressed hers.

"Of course...it does," she bit off. "I've never...felt this way with anyone else."

"Neither have I," he whispered, bending to brush his hard mouth over her soft one. "I told you that when I got home, and I meant it. Never like this, not with any-

one..." His eyes closed, his heavy brows drawing together as he slowly fitted his mouth to hers.

She wanted to protest, but she couldn't move, let
alone speak, and his mouth was making the most exquisite sensations in places far removed from her lips.
With a shaky little sigh she opened her mouth a little to
taste his and felt him stiffen. She felt that same taut-
ness in her legs, her arms, even in her stomach, sensations that she'd never experienced.

His hard fingers flexed, linking with hers caress-
ingly, teasing as he explored her mouth first with his lips
and then with the slightest probing of his tongue.

She hadn't been kissed that way before, and her eyes
opened, puzzled.

He lifted his head a little, searching her face with
green eyes that were dark and mysterious and as full of
answers as her blue ones were full of questions.

"You can trust me this once," he whispered, sensing
her apprehension in the smooth as silk young body that
wouldn't give an inch to the dominance of his. "Even
if I went half mad with wanting, I wouldn't risk trying
to make love to you within sight of the barn."

He couldn't have been less convincing, but she did
trust him. She searched his eyes, feeling the warm
weight of him, smelling the leathery scent that clung to
him, and she began to relax despite the unknown intimacy of the embrace.

"You've never felt a man this way, have you?" he
asked quietly. "It's all right. You're old enough to leave
chaste kisses and daydreams behind. This is the reality,
little Mari," he whispered, shifting his hips as he looked
down into her wide, awed eyes. "This is what it's really
like when a man and a woman come together in pas-

sion. It isn't neat and quiet and uncomplicated. It's hot and wild and complex.''

"Is it part of the rules to warn the victim?" she asked in a husky whisper.

"It is when the victim is as innocent as you," he returned. "I don't want a virgin sacrifice, you see," he added, bending again to her mouth. "I want a full-blooded woman. A woman to match me."

At that moment she almost felt that she could. Her body was throbbing, blazing with fire and fever, and instead of shrinking from the proof of his desire for her, she lifted her body up to his, gave him her mouth and her soft sighs.

Ward felt the hunger in her slender body, and it fostered an oddly protective impulse in him. He, who was used to taking what he wanted without regret or shame, hesitated.

His mouth gentled, slowed and became patiently caressing. He found that she followed where he led, quickly learning the tender lessons that he gave her without words. He let go of her hands and felt them go instinctively to his shirt, pressing over the hard, warm muscles, searching. His heart pounded furiously against breasts whose softness he could feel under him. He wanted to strip off his shirt and give himself to her young hands, he wanted to strip off her own shirt and put his mouth on those tender breasts and look at them and watch her blush. It was then that he realized just how urgent the situation was becoming.

His body was taking over. He could feel himself grinding down against her, forcing her hips into intimate contact with his, he could feel his own taut movements. His mouth felt hot. Hers felt like velvet, feverish and swollen from the hungry probing of his own.

He lifted his head, surprised to find himself breathing in gasps, his arms trembling slightly as they held him poised over her. Her eyes were misty, half closed, her lips parted and moist, her body submissive. His.

She drew in a slow, lazy breath, looking up at him musingly, so hungry for him that she hadn't the strength to refuse him anything he wanted. From the neck down she was throbbing with sweet pulses, experiencing a pleasure that she'd never known before.

"No," he whispered roughly. "No. Not like this."

He rolled away from her, shuddering a little before he sat up and breathed roughly. He brushed back his hair with fingers that were almost steady but held a fine tremor.

Mari was just realizing what had happened, and she stared at him with slowly dawning comprehension. So that was what happened. That was why women didn't fight or protest. It wasn't out of fear of being overpowered. It was because of the sweet, tender pleasure that came from being held intimately, kissed and kissed until her mind got lost in her body's pleasure. He could have had her. But he stopped.

"Surprised?" He turned his head, staring down at her with dark green eyes that still held blatant traces of passion. "I told you I wouldn't take advantage, didn't I?"

"Yes. But I forgot."

"Fortunately for you I didn't." He got to his feet and stretched lazily, feeling as if he'd been beaten, but he wasn't letting her see that. He grinned down at her. "Men get good at pulling back. It comes from years of practice dating virgins," he added in a wicked whisper as he extended a hand to her.

She sat up, flushed, ignoring his outstretched hand as she scrambled to her feet. "I can't imagine that many of them were still virgins afterward," she muttered with a shy glance.

"Oh, some of them had great powers of resistance," he admitted. "Like you."

"Sure," she said shakily, pushing back her damp hair. "Some great resistance. If you hadn't stopped..."

"But I did," he interrupted. He picked up his hat from where he'd tossed it and studied the crown before he put it back on his head. "And for the time being you can forget going back to Georgia," he added with a level gaze. "Lillian needs you. Maybe I need you, too. You've given me a new perspective on things."

"I've butted in and made a spectacle of myself, you mean," she said, her eyes quietly curious on his hard, dark face.

"If I'd meant that, I'd have said it," he returned. "You're a breath of fresh air in my life, Mari. I was getting set in my wicked ways until you came along. Maybe you were right about my attitude toward money. So why don't you stay and reform me?"

"I can't imagine anyone brave enough to try," she said. She lifted her face. "And besides all that, how dare you cost me my job!"

"You can't work in a garage full of men anymore," he said blandly. "Remember your horrible nightmares about the assault?" he added. "Men make you nervous. Lillian said so."

"Those men wouldn't make anyone nervous. All they did was work on cars and go home to their wives," she informed him. "Not one of them was single."

"How sad for you. What wonderful luck that Lillian found me dying and sent for you." He grinned. "It isn't every girl who gets handed a single, handsome, rich bachelor on a platter.''

"I am not a gold digger," she shot at him.

"Oh, hell, I know that," he said after a minute, studying her through narrowed eyes. "But I had to have some kind of defense, didn't I? You're a potent little package, honey. A fish on the hook does fight to the bitter end.''

His words didn't make much sense to her, but Mari was a little dazed by everything that had happened. She just stared at him, puzzled.

"Never mind," he said, taking her hand. "Let's go back. I've got a few odds and ends to take care of before lunch. Do you like to ride?''

"I think so," she admitted.

"You can have your own horse next time," he promised. "But for now I think we'll walk back. I'm just about out of self-control, if you want the truth. I can't handle you at a close proximity right now.''

That was embarrassing and flattering, and she hid a smile. But he saw it and gathered her close to his side, leading the horse by the reins with one hand and holding her with the other. The conversation on the way back was general, but the feel of Ward's strong arm had Mari enthralled every step of the way.

He went off to make some business calls. Lillian took one look at Mari's face and began humming love songs. Mari, meanwhile, went up to her room to freshen up and took time to borrow one of the outside lines to call Atlanta. Her boss at the garage was delighted to hear from her and immediately burst into praise of her unselfishness to help that "poor dying man in Texas." How fortunate, he added brightly, that a young woman about Mari's age had just applied for a job the morning poor Mr. Jessup had called him. Everything had worked out just fine, hadn't it, and how did she like Texas?

She mumbled something about the weather being great for that time of year, thanked him and hung up. Poor Mr. Jessup, indeed!

Ward had to go out on business later in the day, and he wasn't back by supper time. Lillian and Mari ate alone, and after Mari had finished helping in the kitchen, she kissed her aunt good night and went upstairs. She was torn between disappointment and relief that Ward hadn't been home since that feverish interlude. It had been so sweet that she'd wanted it again and that could be dangerous. Each time it got harder to stop. Today she hadn't been able to do anything except follow where he led, and it was like some heady alcoholic beverage—she just couldn't get enough of him. She didn't really know what to do anymore. Her life seemed to be tangled up in complications.

She laid out a soft pink gown on the bed—a warm but revealing one with a low neckline—and fingered it lovingly. It had been an impulse purchase, something to cheer her up on a depressing Saturday when she had been alone. It was made of flannelette, but it was lacy and expensive, and she loved the way it felt and clung to the slender lines of her body.

She ran a bath in the big Jacuzzi and turned on the jets after filling the tub with fragrant soap that was provided, along with anything else a feminine guest might need, in the pretty blue-tiled bathroom. To Mari, who lived in a small efficiency apartment in Atlanta, it was really plush. She frowned as she stripped off her clothing and climbed into the smooth tub with its relaxing jets of water surging around her. The apartment rent was due in a week or so, and she hadn't paid it yet. She'd have to send a check. She also wished that she'd brought more clothes with her. She hadn't counted on being here for life, but it looked as if Ward wasn't in any hurry to let her go.

Too, there was Lillian, who was behaving herself only as long as her niece was around to make her. If Mari left, what would happen to the older woman? With Ward away on business so often, it was dangerous for Lillian to be left alone now. Perhaps Ward had considered that, and it was why he wanted Mari to stay. The real reason, anyway. He didn't seem to be dying of love for her, although his desire was apparent. He wanted her.

With all her turbulent thoughts and the humming sound of the Jacuzzi, she didn't hear the door to her room open or hear it close again. She didn't hear the soft footfalls on the carpet, or the soft sound that came from a particularly male voice as Ward saw her sitting up in the tub with her pretty pink breasts bare and glistening with soap and water.

She happened to glance up then and saw him. She couldn't move. His green eyes were steady and loving on the soft curves of her body, and with horror she felt the tips of her breasts harden under his intent scrutiny.

He shook his head when she started to lift her hands to them. "No," he said gently, moving toward her. "No, don't cover them, Mari."

She could hardly get her breath. Although she'd never let anyone see her like this in all her life, she couldn't stop him. Mari couldn't seem to move at all. He towered over her, still and somber, and as she watched, he began to roll up the sleeves of the white shirt that was open halfway down his chest. He'd long ago shed his jacket and tie, although he was still wearing dress boots and suit trousers. He looked expensive and very masculine and disturbing, and as he bent beside the tub, she caught the scent of luxurious cologne.

"You mustn't!" she began frantically.

But he picked up the big fluffy sponge she'd soaped and shook his head, smiling faintly. "Think of it as a service for a special, tired guest," he whispered amusedly, although his eyes were frankly possessive. "Lie back and enjoy it."

She started to protest again, but he didn't pay the least attention. One lean hand moved behind her neck to support her in the bubbling water while the other slowly, painstakingly, drew the sponge over every soft line and curve of her body.

She hadn't realized how many nerve endings she had, but he found every single one. In a silence that throbbed with new sensation, he bathed her, pausing now and again to put the sponge down and touch her, experience the softness of her skin with the added silkiness of soap and water making it vibrantly alive.

Her eyes were half closed, languorous, as his fingers brushed lightly over her small, high breasts and found every curve and hardness, every sensual contrast, every texture, as if she fascinated him.

She trembled a little when he turned off the Jacuzzi and let the water out of the tub, especially when he began to sponge away the last traces of soap, and her body was completely revealed to him.

He lifted his dark, quiet eyes to hers and searched them, finding apprehension, fear, awe and delight in their blue depths. "I've never bathed a woman before," he said softly. "Or bathed with one. In some ways I suppose I'm pretty old-fashioned."

She was breathing unsteadily. "I've never let anyone look at me before," she said in a hesitant tone.

"Yes. I know." He helped her out of the tub and removed a warmed towel from the rail. It was fluffy and pink, and warm against her skin as he slowly dried her from head to toe. This time she could feel his hands in a new way, and she clutched at his broad shoulders when he reached her hips and began to touch her flat stomach. She felt a rush of sensation that was new and shocking.

"Ward?" she whispered.

He knelt in front of her, discarding the towel and all pretense as he held her hips and pressed his mouth warmly against her stomach.

She cried out. It was a high-pitched, helpless cry, and it made his blood surge like a flood through his veins. His fingers flexed and his mouth drew over her stomach with agonizing slowness, moving up with relentless hunger to her soft, smooth breasts.

She held him there, held his hard, moist mouth over the tip of one, felt him take her inside, warming her. He touched her then in a way she'd never expected, and her breath drew in harshly and she shivered.

"Shhhh," he whispered at her breast. "It's all right. Don't fight me."

She couldn't have. She shuddered and trembled, crying as he made the most exquisite sensations felt in the nether reaches of her slender body. Her nails dug into him and she couldn't help it.

"Marianne," he whispered, shifting his mouth over hers. He stopped his delicate probing and lifted her in his arms. She felt the soft shock of his footsteps as he carried her to the bed, felt the mattress sink under their combined weights.

His mouth moved slowly back down her to her stomach, her thighs, and then she did fight him, fought the newness and the strangeness and the frank intimacy.

He lifted his head and slid back up to look at her shocked face. "All right," he said gently. "If you don't want it, I won't force you."

Her face was creamy pink now, fascinated. He looked down at her body, smoothing over it with a lean, very dark hand, savoring its soft vulnerability.

"This is so new," he whispered. "I never realized how soft a woman's body really was, how exquisitely formed. I could get drunk just on the sight of you."

She was trembling all over but not from the soft chill of the room. She felt reckless under his intense gaze.

He looked up into her eyes. "You aren't protected, are you?" he asked softly.

It took a minute for her to realize what he was asking, and it made the situation take on alarming, very adult implications. To him this was familiar territory. But Mari was a pioneer.

"No," she whispered unsteadily. "I'm not."

"It's just as well," he murmured, bending to her mouth. "I think...it might spoil things right now to force that kind of total intimacy on you." His hand smoothed tenderly over her breast as he probed at her trembling lips. "Don't you want to touch me like this?"

She did, but she couldn't say it. Her hands went slowly to his shirt and slid under it, finding the exciting abrasion of thick chest hair over warm muscle a heady combination. His mouth moved hungrily against hers at the first tentative touch, and one hand went between them to rip the fabric completely out of the way and give her total access.

His harsh breathing disturbed her, but she was intoxicated by the intimacy they were sharing. Impulsively she moved her hands and arched upward letting her breasts tease his chest, feeling the sudden acceleration of his heartbeat with wonder.

He poised over her, lifting his head. His eyes were dark with passion, his chest shuddering with it. "Do that again," he said roughly.

She did, on fire with hunger, wanting something more than the teasing, wanting him. She felt his chest tremble, and she looked down at his darkness against her paler flesh with a sense of wonder.

"Yes, look at it," he whispered, his voice harsh, shaken as he stared, too. "Look at the differences. Dark against light, muscle against softness. Your breasts are like bread and honey."

As he spoke, he eased down. His heavy body surged against hers as he fitted it over her bareness, and her pupils dilated helplessly at the warm ecstasy of his full weight over her.

"Give me your mouth now," he whispered, bending. "Let me feel you completely."

It was a kiss like nothing she'd ever imagined in her life. She held him tenderly, her hands smoothing his thick, dark hair, her body throbbing its whole length where she could feel the powerful muscles of his body taut and smooth.

He tasted of coffee, and there was a new tenderness in him, in the lips that delicately pushed at hers so that his tongue could enter the soft, sweet darkness of her mouth. She felt it touch hers, tangle with it, and she gave herself up to a sensation that was all mystery and delight.

His hands smoothed down her sides, her back, savoring the smooth suppleness of her skin. He ached like hell, and he could have cursed himself for causing this, for forgetting how naive she was. She wanted him and, God, he wanted her! But he could make her pregnant. And part of her would hate him forever if he forced this on her. It wasn't going to be good for her. She was so much a virgin . . .

His cheek slid against hers, and he rolled onto his side, holding her protectively to him, feeling her breasts crush softly against his chest.

"Hold me," he whispered. "Just hold me until we stop trembling."

"I want you," she whimpered, beyond thought, beyond pride. She bit his shoulder. "I want you."

"I know. But we can't." His cheek nuzzled hers, and his lips touched her tear-streaked face tenderly. He hadn't realized she was crying until then. He drew a breath. "Are you all right?" he asked softly.

"I ache," she sobbed.

"I could satisfy you," he whispered. "Without going all the way."

She sensed that. Her eyes searched his in wonder. "No," she said after a minute. "I won't do that to you." She touched his face, fascinated by the look the words produced. "I'm sorry. I should have said something a long time ago. I should have asked you to stop."

"But it was too sweet, wasn't it?" he asked, his voice quiet and deep as he touched her face with fingers that were possessive and gentle. "So sweet, like making love with every part of us. I've never in my life experienced anything like it. Not even sex was ever this good."

That shocked her, and her eyes mirrored it. "Not . . . even sex?"

He shook his head. "With you I think it would be lovemaking, not sex. I don't think you and I could accept something as coldly clinical as that."

She was so tempted. She wanted him desperately. Everybody did it these days, didn't they? Maybe she wouldn't get pregnant. She loved him. Loved him!

But he saw the uncertainty in her eyes and mistook it for fear. For God's sake, where was his brain, anyway? She was a virgin. Lillian was right downstairs. Was he crazy? He ignored the feverish hunger of his body and managed to smile reassuringly as he slowly drew away from her to sit up with a hard sigh.

"No more, honey," he said heavily and managed to laugh. "I'm too old for this kind of playing."

Playing? She stared at him helplessly as he forced his staggered brain to function and found her gown. He put her into it with a minimum of fuss and then lifted her long enough to turn down the covers. He put her under them, smoothing them over her breasts.

He couldn't tell her that his own vulnerability and weakness had shocked him. He hadn't planned this, he hadn't expected to be drawn into such a long, intimate loving. It had been loving, of a kind. He scowled, watching her, fascinated by her innocence, her helpless reaction to his touch. He'd come to her room, in fact, to tell her that he wanted to get on a friendly footing with her, to stop the intimacy that could all too easily overwhelm both of them. But the sight of her in that tub had wiped every sane thought right out of his mind. Now he looked at her and saw commitment and the loss of his precious freedom. He saw all the old wounds, the helplessness of his attraction to that tramp who'd taken him in.

With a rough curse he got to his feet, running an angry hand through his hair.

"You needn't look at me that way," she bit off, close to tears again but for a totally different reason. "As if I were a fallen woman. I didn't walk into your bathroom and start staring at you."

"I didn't mean for that to happen," he said curtly.

She softened a little at the confession. He looked as shaken as she felt. "It's all right," she replied, fumbling with the coverlet. "I didn't, either."

"I'm old enough to know better, though," he murmured, feeling venerable and protective as he stared down at her. He put his hands in his pockets with a long sigh. "I came up here to see if we might get on a different footing. A friendly footing, without all these physical complications." He laughed softly. "I suppose you noticed how well I succeeded."

"Yes," she murmured tongue in cheek. She recalled everything she'd let him do and went scarlet, dropping her embarrassed eyes.

"None of that," he chided. "You're a woman now, not a little girl. Nothing we did would make you pregnant."

"I know that!" she burst out, feverishly avoiding his mocking gaze.

"I just wanted to reassure you." He stretched lazily, very masculine with his shirt unbuttoned and his hair mussed. Very disturbing, watching her that way. "No one will ever know what we did in here," he added. "Just you and me. That makes it a very private thing, Mari."

"Yes." She glanced up and then down again. "I hope you don't think I do that with just anyone."

"I don't think that at all." He bent and brushed his lips gently over her forehead. "It's very exciting being the first," he whispered. "Even in this way."

Her face felt hot as she looked up into lazy, warm eyes. "I'm glad it was with you."

"Yes. So am I." He searched her eyes gently and started to lean toward her, but his survival instincts warned him against it. Instead, he stood up with a smile and went to the door. "Good night, honey. Sleep well."

"You, too."

He closed the door without looking back, and Mari stared at it for a long time before she drew a shuddering sigh and turned out the light.

Chapter Eight

Mari hardly slept. She felt his hands all through the night, along with a new and curious kind of frustration that wouldn't subside. Every time she thought about Ward, her body began to throb. These new feelings frightened her because they were so unexpected. She didn't know what to do. The urge to cut and run was very strong.

Lillian was hobbling around putting platters on the table for breakfast. She looked up, smiling, as Mari came into the room dressed in jeans and a pullover burgundy knit blouse.

"Good morning, glory," Lillian said brightly. "Isn't it a beautiful day?"

It was, in fact, but Lillian seemed to be overjoyed at something besides the great outdoors. "Yes," Mari returned. She glanced at the empty chair at the head of the table.

"He'll be back in a minute," the older woman said knowingly. "Looks like a storm cloud this morning, he does. All ruffled and absentminded. Been staring up that staircase ever since he came downstairs, too," she added wickedly.

Mari darted into the kitchen. "I'll help you get breakfast on the table," she said quickly, avoiding that amused gaze. At least Lillian was enjoying herself. Mari wasn't. She was afraid.

She and Lillian had started eating before Ward came back. He looked tired, but his face brightened when he spotted Mari. He smiled without really wanting to and tossed his hat onto a side table before he sprawled into a chair. His jeans were dusty and his blue checked shirt was a little disheveled.

"I've washed up," he told Lillian before she could open her mouth. "I had to help get a bull out of a ditch."

"How did he get into the ditch?" Mari asked curiously.

Ward grinned. "Trying to jump a fence to get to one of my young heifers. Amazing how love affects the mind, isn't it?"

Mari flushed. Lillian giggled. Ward leaned back in his chair, enjoying the view, watching Mari try to eat scrambled eggs with forced enjoyment.

"Don't you want something to eat, boss?" Lillian asked.

"I'm not really hungry," he said without realizing what he was giving away to the old woman, who beamed at him. "But I'll have some toast and coffee, I guess. Sleep well, Mari?" he asked as Lillian handed him the carafe.

Mari lifted her eyes. "Of course," she said, bluffing. "Did you?"

He shook his head, smiling faintly. "Not a wink."

She got lost in his green gaze and felt the force of it all the way to her toes. It took several seconds to drag her eyes down to her plate, and even then her heart ran wild.

Ward watched her with evident enjoyment, caught up in the newness of having a woman react that way to his teasing. Everything was new with Marianne. Just ordinary things, like sharing breakfast, took on new dimensions. He found that he liked looking at her. Especially now since he knew exactly what she looked like under her clothes. His eyes darkened in memory. God, how exquisite she was!

Mari felt his intent stare all through her body. She could have made a meal of him, too, with her eyes. He looked so good. For all his huge size he was lithe and graceful, and she loved the way he moved. He was as sensuous a man as she'd ever known, a very masculine presence with a disturbing effect on her senses. She didn't think her feet would ever touch the ground again. Just being near him set her on fire. She wanted to get up and touch him, put her mouth on his, feel his arms crushing her to every inch of that long, elegant body. Her fingers trembled on her fork, and she flushed with embarrassment when he noticed her nervousness.

"Come for a ride with me," Ward said suddenly.

She looked up at him. "Now?"

He shrugged. "Lillian can answer the phone. There's nothing pressing for today. Why not?"

"No reason at all," Lillian agreed quickly. "Go ahead. I'll handle the home front."

Mari submitted before she could begin to protest. Why pretend? She wanted to be alone with him, and he knew it. Her blue eyes searched his green ones longingly, everything plain and undisguised in her oval face. He felt explosive. Young. A boy again with a special girl.

He threw down his napkin and got to his feet, hoping his helpless urgency didn't show too much. "Let's go," he bit off.

Mari followed him. She barely heard Lillian's voice behind her saying something about having fun. Her eyes were on Ward's strong back, her body moving as if she were a sleepwalker. She was on fire for him. Whatever happened now happened. She loved him. If he wanted her, she wasn't going to stop him. He had to feel something for her, too. He had to care just a little!

He saddled two horses in stark silence, his hands deft and firm as he pulled cinches tight and checked bridles.

When he helped her into the saddle, his eyes were dark and possessive, his hand lingering when she was seated. "You look good on a horse, honey," he said quietly.

She looked down at him and smiled, feeling the warmth of his chest against her leg. "Do I?" she asked gently, her voice soft with longing.

"I want you, Marianne," he said half under his breath. "I've thought about nothing else all night. So go slow, will you? I want to talk today. Just talk. I want to get to know you."

That was flattering and a little surprising. Maybe even disappointing. But she had to keep it from showing so she kept smiling. "I'd like that," she said.

He didn't answer her. He felt the same hunger she did, but he was more adept at hiding his yearnings. He didn't want to frighten her off, not before he made a stab at establishing a relationship with her. He didn't know how she was going to react to what he had in mind, but he knew they couldn't go on like this. Things had to be settled—today. Business was going to suffer if he kept on mooning over that perfect young body. Physical attraction was a damnable inconvenience, he thought angrily. He'd thought he was too old to be this susceptible. Apparently he was more vulnerable than he'd ever realized.

He swung into the saddle and led the way down the long trail that ran around the ranch. His men were out working with the cattle, getting them moved to summer pasture, doing all the little things around the ranch that contributed to the huge cow-calf operation. Fixing machines. Planting feed. Cleaning out stalls. Checking supplies. Making lists of chores. It was a big task, running a ranch even this size, but Ty Wade's, which adjoined it, was huge by comparison. The oil business was Ward's main concern, but he did like the idea of running cattle, as his grandfather had done so many years before. Perhaps it got into a man's blood. Not that he minded sinking wells under his cattle. He had one or two on his own property, and Tyson Wade's spread was proving to be rich in the black gold. His instincts hadn't failed him there, and he was glad. Ty would never have let him live it down if he'd been wrong and the oil hadn't been there. As it was, the discovery on that leased land had saved Ty from some hard financial times. It had worked out well all the way around.

Mari glanced at him, curious about that satisfied look on his hard, dark face. She wondered what thoughts were giving him such pleasure.

He laughed out loud, staring ahead. "Those old instincts never seem to let me down," he murmured. "I think I could find oil with my nose."

"What?"

He looked over at her. "I was thinking about that oil I found on Ty Wade's place. It was a hell of a gamble, but it sure paid off."

So. It was business that made him feel so good, not her company. "Is business the only pleasure in your life?" she asked gently.

He shrugged. "The only lasting one, I guess." He stared toward the horizon. "There were some pretty hard times around here when I was a kid. Oh, we always had plenty of food, you know—that's one of the advantages of living on a ranch. But we didn't have much in the way of material things. Clothes were all secondhand, and I wore boots with holes in the soles for most of my childhood. That wasn't so bad, but I got ragged a lot about my mother."

She could imagine that he had. "I guess I was pretty lucky," she said. "My parents were good to me. We always got by."

He studied her quietly. "I'll bet you were a tomboy."

She laughed, delighted. "I was. I played sandlot baseball and climbed trees and played war. There was only one other girl on my street, and she and I had to be tough to survive with all the boys. They didn't pull their punches just because we were girls. We had a good time growing up all the same."

He fingered the reins as they rode along to the musical squeak of saddle leather. "I liked playing cowboys and Indians," he recalled. "Had my own horse."

"Which were you?"

He chuckled. "Mostly I was the Indian. I had a Cherokee ancestor, they say."

"You're very dark," she agreed.

"Honey, that's sun, not inherited. I spent a lot of time working rigs when I was younger, and I still help out on occasion. The heat's easier stripped to the waist."

She'd noticed how dark his skin was when he'd stripped off his shirt the night before and let her touch him. Her eyes went involuntarily to the hard muscles of his torso and lingered there.

"You don't do much sunbathing, do you?" he asked unexpectedly, and his eyes told her that he was remembering how pale she was.

Her face colored. "No. There's no beach nearby, and I live upstairs in an apartment building. I don't have any place to sunbathe."

"It isn't good for the skin. Mine's like leather," he commented. "Yours is silky soft...."

She urged her mount ahead, embarrassed because she knew what he was seeing in his mind.

His mount fell into easy step beside her. "Don't be shy with me," he said gently. "There's nothing to be ashamed of."

"I guess I seem grass green to you," she commented.

"Sure you do," he replied and smiled. "I like it."

Her eyes went to the flat horizon beyond, to the scant trees and the long fence lines and the red coats of the cattle. "I never had many boyfriends," she told him, remembering. "My dad was very strict."

"What was he like?"

"Oh, very tall and stubborn. And terrific," she added. "I had great parents. I loved them both. Losing

Mama was hard, but having both of them gone is really rough. I never missed having brothers or sisters until now.''

"I suppose it makes you feel alone."

"I've felt that way for a long time," she said. "My father wasn't really an affectionate man, and he didn't like close ties. He thought it was important that I stand alone. Perhaps he was right. I got used to being by myself after Mama died."

He studied her averted features. "At least I had Grandmother and Belinda," he said. "Although with Grandmother it's been a fight all the way. She's too much like me."

She remembered him saying that the only women he cared about where those two. "What is your sister like?" she asked.

He grinned. "Like Grandmother and me. She's another hardheaded Jessup."

"Does she look like you?" she asked curiously.

"Not a lot. Same green eyes, but she's prettier, and we're built differently."

She glared at him. "I do realize that."

"No. She's small. Petite," he clarified. "I suppose I take after my father. He was a big man."

"An oilman?"

He nodded. "Always looking for that big strike." His eyes suddenly had a faraway look. "Right out there is where we found him, in that grove of trees." He gestured to the horizon. "Hell of a shock. There was hardly a mark on him. He looked like he was asleep."

"I'm sorry."

"It was a long time ago." He turned his horse, leaving her to follow where the trail led down to the river and a grove of trees. He dismounted, tying his horse to

a small tree growing on a grassy knoll. He helped Mari
down and tied hers nearby.

"Funny, I never thought of Texas being like this,"
she mused as she watched the shallow river run over the
rocks and listened to its serene bubbling. "It's so bare
except for occasional stands of timber. Along the
streams, of course, there are more trees. But it's not at
all what I expected. It's so... big."

"Georgia doesn't look like this?" he asked.

She watched him stretch out on the leaves under a big
live oak tree, his body relaxed as he studied her. "Not
a lot, no. We don't have mesquite trees," she said.
"Although around Savannah we do have huge live oaks
like these. Near Atlanta we have lots of dogwoods and
maples and pines, but there's not so much open land.
There are always trees on the horizon, except in south
Georgia. I guess southwest Georgia is a lot like here.
I've even seen prickly pear cactus growing there, and
there are diamondback rattlers in that part of the state.
I had a great aunt there when I was a child. I still remember visiting her."

He drew up a knee and crossed his arms, leaning back
against the tree. "Homesick yet?"

"Not really," she confessed shyly. "I always wanted
to visit a real ranch. I guess I got my wish." She turned.
"Do you think Aunt Lillian will be all right now?"

"Yes, I do." He laughed. "She's having a hell of a
good time with us. You haven't told her that we know
the truth about each other?"

"No," she said. "I didn't want to disappoint her. But
we really ought to tell her."

"Not yet." He let his darkening eyes run down her
body, and his blood began to run hot. "Come here."

She gnawed her lower lip. "I don't think that's a good idea," she began half convincingly.

"Like hell you don't," he returned. "You didn't sleep last night any more than I did, and I'll bet your heart is doing the same tango mine is."

It was, but she was apprehensive. Last night it had been so difficult to stop.

"You want me, Marianne," he said under his breath. "And God knows, I want you. We're alone. No prying eyes. No one to see or hear what we do together. Make love with me."

Her mind kept saying no. So why did her legs carry her to him? She couldn't hear reason through the wild slamming of her heart at her throat. She needed him like water in the desert, like warmth in the cold.

He opened his arms, and she went down into them. Coming home. Feeling his big body warm and close to hers, his arms protecting, his eyes possessive.

He rolled over, taking her with him until she was lying on her back under the shade of the big tree with its soft green leaves blowing in the warm breeze.

As she watched, his hand went to his shirt. He flicked open the buttons until his chest was bare, and then his hand went to the hem of her blouse. She caught his wrist, but it didn't even slow him down. He slid his hand under it and around to the back, easily undoing the catch of her bra.

"Why bother with that thing?" he whispered, sliding his hand around to tease the side of her breast. "It just gets in my way."

Her body trembled at the lazy brushing of his fingers. "Why can't I fight you?" she whispered huskily.

"Because what we give each other defies reason," he whispered. He looked down at her mouth as his fingers brushed closer and closer to the hard, aching tip of her breast. "Little virgin, you excite me beyond bearing, do you know that? I can feel what this does to you. Here..."

His forefinger touched the hard tip and she gasped, shuddering under him, her eyes huge and frightened.

"My God, you can't imagine what it does to me," he said curtly. "Feeling that and knowing that I'm causing it. Knowing how hungry you are for me. If I took you right now, you'd scream, Marianne. You'd writhe and cry out, and I wouldn't be able to hold back a damned thing because you've already got me so aroused I don't know where I am."

As he spoke, he moved, letting her feel the proof of the statement as his weight settled against her. His big hand smoothed up, cupping her warm breast, and his mouth opened, taking her lips with it in a silence that shattered her resistance.

Her body lifted toward him as he slid both hands under it, taking her breasts, savoring them with his warm, calloused hands. His mouth was taking a wild toll of hers, crushing against her parted lips, tasting the sweetness of them in a blazing hunger.

Her hips shifted and he groaned huskily. Her eyes opened, looking curiously up into his.

"What you feel is getting worse by the minute," he whispered huskily. "If you start moving your hips, I'm going to lose control. Are you willing to take that risk?"

She almost was. Her body was crying out for fulfillment. She wanted his hands on all of her. She wanted his clothes out of the way so that she could touch his skin. She wanted to smooth her fingers down the hard muscles of his back and thighs and feel him in the most intimate embrace of all.

He groaned at the look in her eyes. His hand found hers, pulling it to his body, pressing it flat against him, letting her experience him.

She trembled and jerked away from that intimacy, and it brought him to his senses. He rolled over, bringing up his legs, covering his eyes with his forearms. He stiffened, groaning harshly.

"I'm sorry," she whispered, biting her lip. "Ward, I'm sorry!"

"Not your fault," he managed roughly. His teeth clenched. "God, it hurts!"

She sat up, helpless. She didn't know what to do, what to say. It must be horrible for him, and it was her fault, and she didn't know how to ease that obvious pain.

He jackknifed to a sitting position, bent over his drawn-up legs, breathing unsteadily. His hands were clenched together, and the knuckles went white. He shuddered and let out an uneven breath.

"I never realized . . . it hurt men like that," she faltered. "I'm so sorry!"

"I told you it's not your fault," he said curtly. He didn't look at her. He couldn't yet. His body was still in torment, but it was easing just a little. He sat quietly, waiting for the ache to go away. She was potent. He wondered if he was ever going to be able to stand up again. Damn his principles and damn hers!

"If I were modern and sophisticated . . ." she began angrily.

"That's what we're going to talk about in a minute," he said.

She stared at his downbent head, absently fumbling to close her bra and pull down her blouse. Together they were an explosive pair. She loved him beyond bearing.

Did he, could he, feel the same way? Her heart flew up into the sun. Was he going to ask her to marry him?

She scrambled to her feet, feeling nervous and shy and on the edge of some monumental discovery. "What are we going to talk about?" she asked, her eyes bright, her smile shy and soft.

He looked up, catching his breath at the beauty in her face. "I want you."

"Yes, I know."

He smiled slowly. "I guess you do, honey," he said, reminding her of that forbidden touch that made her blush.

She lowered her eyes to the ground, watching an ant make its way across a twig. "Well?"

"We can't go on like this," he said, getting slowly to his feet. He stopped just in front of her, near the edge of the river. "You realize that, don't you?"

"Yes," she said miserably.

"And one of these days I'm going to go off my head. It could have happened just now. Men aren't too reliable when their bodies start getting that involved," he added quietly. "I'm just like any other man in passion. I want fulfillment."

She swallowed. This was it. She looked up. "So. What do you want to do about it?" she asked gently.

He stuck his hands into his pockets and searched her eyes with a weary sigh. "I'll set you up in an apartment for a start," he said, his voice reluctant but firm. "I'll open an expense account for you, give you whatever you need. Lillian can be told that you've got a job in the city. Not Ravine, obviously. Maybe in Victoria. That's not too far away for me to drive, and it's big enough that people won't be too curious."

She stared at him. "But it's so far from the ranch..." she began, wondering how they were going to stay married with that kind of arrangement.

"Far enough to keep people from making remarks," he said. "I don't want to expose you to gossip."

"Gossip?" She blinked. Wasn't he proposing?

"You know how I feel about my freedom," he said curtly. "I can't give that up. But you'll have a part of my life that I've never shared with anyone else. You'll never want for anything. And there won't be another woman. Not ever. Just you. I'll manage enough time to keep us both happy when we're together."

It was all becoming clear now. His hard face and his determined eyes gave her all the information she needed.

"You're asking me to be your mistress." She almost choked on the word, but she had to be sure.

He nodded, confirming her worst fears. "That's all I can give you, Marianne. That's all I have to give. Marriage isn't something I want. I've had a taste of commitment that left me half demented. I'll never risk it again."

"And you think that I can be satisfied with this kind of arrangement?" she asked in a ghost of her normal voice.

"You'll be satisfied, all right," he said, his voice sensual and low. "I'll satisfy you to the roots of your hair, little virgin."

"And...Aunt Lillian?"

He shifted uncomfortably. Somehow this was all leaving a bad taste in his mouth. It had seemed the right thing, the only thing, to do when he'd worked it out last night. But now it sounded and felt cheap.

"Lillian will never have to know," he said shortly.

"And what if I get pregnant?" she asked blatantly. "Nothing is foolproof."

He drew in a slow breath. Children. He hadn't realized that children might come of such a liaison. He studied her, wondering absently if they might have a son together. His body surged in a new and unexpected way. His reaction shocked him.

"Pregnant." He said the word aloud, savoring it.

"It does happen," she reminded him, going colder by the second. "Or hasn't the problem ever arisen before?" she added, wondering how many women had come and gone in his life.

"I've never been desperate enough to compromise a virgin before," he said quietly, searching her eyes. "I've never wanted anything the way I want you."

She pulled herself erect. "I'm sorry," she said stiffly. "Sorry that you think so little of me that you could make a proposition like that. I guess I've given you every reason to think I'd accept, and I'm sorry for that, too. I never realized how...how easy it would make me seem to you."

His face fell. He could feel his heart sinking. "Cheap?" he asked softly. "Marianne, that's the last thing I think of you!"

"Do tell?" She laughed through building tears. "I'll bet you've made that little speech until it's second nature to you! I'll bet you've even forgotten the names of the women you've had in your bed!"

His lips parted on a caught breath. This wasn't working out the way he'd envisioned. Nothing was going right. There were tears in her eyes, for God's sake.

"Marianne, don't . . ." he began, reaching for her.

"Don't you touch me, Ward Jessup," she sobbed, sidestepping. "I've made an awful fool of myself, and I guess you had every reason to ask me what you did, but I don't want to be any rich man's kept woman, thanks."

"Look here—" He started toward her again.

Instinctively her hands went out, and she pushed jerkily at his chest. Ordinarily it wouldn't have moved him. But the riverbank was slick, and his boots went out from under him. He went over backward with a horrible splash.

Mari didn't stay around to see how wet he was. She ran for her horse, fumbled for the reins from around the trunk of the tree and struggled into the saddle through a blur of tears.

Ward stood up, dripping wet, watching her ride away. He didn't think he'd ever in his life felt so miserable or so stupid. It had seemed like a good idea, that proposition. He didn't want marriage, he didn't. For God's sake, why did women have to have so much permanence? Why couldn't they just enjoy themselves like men did? Then he thought about Mari "enjoying" herself with another man, and his face went ruddy with bad temper. He didn't understand himself lately. But the sight of her riding away, almost certainly to a speedy departure from the ranch, made him feel hollow inside.

Mari rode home feeling just as hollow herself. She should have been flattered, she supposed, at such a generous offer. But she only felt cheap. Stupid, she told herself. You let him do whatever he wants and then get angry at him for making the obvious assumption. She hated herself for giving in, for giving him license to such intimacy. Her body had betrayed her, hungry for pleasure, and she'd lost her reason somewhere along the way. Now she was going to have to leave here. All because she hadn't been sensible. All because she loved him too much to deny herself the ecstasy of his love-making.

"You've got a lot to answer for," she told her body angrily. She could have died of shame. Now he'd be sure that she was an idiot.

What was she going to tell Lillian? Her heart sank. The older woman would be heartbroken. Mari closed her eyes, feeling the tears burn them. Why had she ever come here? It had begun so sweetly, only to end in such tragedy. Well, she'd made her bed. Now she'd have to try to lie in it. That wouldn't be much comfort in the lonely years ahead. Leaving Ward Jessup behind would hurt more than anything else ever had. She'd loved him too much, and now she was going to lose him because of it. Because he didn't want commitment and she did.

Perhaps she should have said yes, she thought miserably. Then she thought about how she'd feel, being kept, being used and then abandoned. No. It was better to never know him that way than to have a taste of him and lose him. It would only make things worse, and she'd never respect herself again. Oddly enough, she had a feeling that he wouldn't have respected her, either. Pride would get her through, she promised herself. Yes. She still had that, even if her heart was shattered. She lifted her face and dried the tears on her sleeve. She had to think up some good excuse to go back to Georgia. Something that would give Lillian a reason to think she'd be back, which would keep her on the mend. Her eyes narrowed in deep thought as she approached the ranch house.

Chapter Nine

Mari thought she had it down pat when she left her horse with one of the men at the stable and went into the house to tell Lillian she was leaving.

The older woman was sitting down in the living room, looking smug while she thumbed through a magazine.

Mari paused in the hall, took a deep breath and went into the room determinedly. "Well," she said brightly, "I've got a terrific assignment!"

"You've what?" Lillian asked, staring at her niece.

"Mr. Jessup is sending me to Atlanta to get some information on a distant relative of his," she continued, pretending for all she was worth. "You know, to go into his memoirs. It will give me a chance to see about my rent at the apartment and get some more clothes, too."

Lillian had stiffened, but she relaxed all at once with a smile. "Just for a few days, I guess?" she probed.

"That's right." Mari sighed, laying it on thick. "Isn't he just the nicest man? What a pity he's got so little time." She peeked at Lillian out of the corner of one eye. "There's not much sense in getting attached to a dying man, you know."

Lillian hadn't considered that. She gnawed her lip thoughtfully. "He's not a goner yet," she said. "He could get well." She warmed to her topic. "That's right. They could find a treatment that would work and save him!"

"That would be lovely. He's so macho, you know," Mari said with a forced smile.

"Isn't he, though? You two seem to be spending quite a lot of time together these days, too," she added. "Exchanging some very interesting looks as well."

Mari lowered her eyes demurely. "He's very handsome."

"You're very pretty." Lillian put the magazine aside. "When are you going to Atlanta?"

"This very afternoon!" Mari enthused. "I want to hurry and get back," she added.

Lillian fell for it, hook, line and sinker. "Is he going to let you fly there?" she asked.

"No, I'm, uh, taking the bus. Hate flying, you know. Just do it when I have to." Actually, she didn't have the price of a ticket, thanks to her lost job and small savings account. It would take all she had to pay her rent, and then she'd have to pray that she could find another job. Damn Ward Jessup!

"Bus?" Lillian began, giving her suspicious looks.

"He'll come after me, of course," she said. "We might drive back...."

The older woman brightened. Lots of opportunities if they had to stop overnight. Of course, they wouldn't do anything reckless. She knew Mari wouldn't.

"Do you need some help packing?" she asked Mari.

"No, thanks, dear, I can do it. And I'd better get busy!" She blew Aunt Lillian a kiss. "You'll be all right until I get back?" she added, hesitating.

"Of course," Lillian huffed. "I just have a broken leg. I'm taking those stupid pills."

"Good." Mari went upstairs and quickly threw things into her bag. She called the bus station to ask about an outgoing bus and was delighted to find that she had an hour to get to the station. She grabbed her bag and rushed back down the staircase just in time to watch a wet, angry, coldly polite Ward Jessup come in the front door.

"I told Aunt Lillian about the job, Mr. Jessup," she said, loud enough for Lillian to hear. "My goodness, what happened to you? You're all wet!"

Ward glared at her. "So I am, Miss Raymond," he returned. His gaze went to the bag in her hand. Well, he'd expected it, hadn't he? What did she think he'd do, propose marriage?

Mari went the rest of the way down the staircase, keeping her features calm when she felt like throwing herself at his wet boots and begging him to let her stay. She did have a little pride left. Anyway, he was the one who should be ashamed of himself, going around propositioning good girls.

"Boss, you'd better get into some dry clothes," Lillian fussed.

"I will in a minute." He glared at Mari. "When do you leave?"

"In an hour. Can you get somebody to run me to the bus station? After all, the research trip," she raised her voice, "was your idea."

"Tell Billy I said to drive you," he said curtly, and his eyes cut into hers.

"I'll do that," she replied, struggling to maintain her tattered pride. Her hands clutched the bag. "See you."

He didn't reply. Lillian was getting suspicious.

"Aren't you going to drive her?" Lillian asked him.

"He's soaking wet, poor thing," Mari reminded her. "You wouldn't want him to get worse."

"No, of course not!" Lillian said quickly. "But should you go alone, Mari, with your bad experience."

"She's tough," Ward told his housekeeper, and his eyes were making furious statements in the privacy of the hallway. "She'll get by."

"You bet I will, big man," she assured him. "Better luck next time," she added under her breath. "Sorry I wasn't more...cooperative."

"Don't miss your bus, honey," he said in a tone as cold as snow.

She smiled prettily and went past him to kiss Lillian goodbye.

Lillian frowned as she returned the hug. "Are you sure nothing's wrong?"

"Not a thing," Mari said and smiled convincingly. "He's just trying not to show how hurt he is that I'm leaving," she added in a whisper.

"Oh," Lillian said, although she was feeling under-currents.

"See you soon," Mari promised. She walked straight past Ward, who was quietly dripping on the hall carpet, his fists clenched by his side. "So long, boss," she drawled. "Don't catch cold, now."

"If I die of pneumonia, I hope your conscience hurts you," he muttered.

She turned at the doorway. "It's more likely that pneumonia would catch you and die. You're dripping on the carpet."

"It's my damned carpet. I'll drip on it if I please."

She searched his hard eyes, seeing nothing welcoming or tender there now. The lover of an hour ago might never have been. "I'll give Georgia your regards."

"Have you got enough money for a bus ticket?" he asked.

She glared at him. "If I didn't have it," she said under her breath, "I'd wait tables to get it! I don't want your money!"

He was learning that the hard way. As he tried to find the right words to smooth over the hurt, to stop her until he could sort out his puzzling, disturbing new feelings, she whirled and went out the door.

"She sure is in a temper." Lillian sighed as she hobbled out of the living room and down the hall. "Sure is going to be lonesome around here without her." She stopped and turned, her eyes full of regret and resignation. "I guess you know what I told her."

"I know," he said curtly. "Everything."

She shrugged. "I was getting older. She was alone. I just wanted her to have somebody to care about her. I'm sorry. I hope both of you can forgive me. I'll write Mari and try to explain. No sense trying to talk to her right now." She knew something had gone badly wrong between them, and the boss didn't look any more eager to discuss it than Mari had. "I hope you'll forgive me."

"I already have."

She looked up with a wan smile. "She's not a bad girl. You . . . will let her come back if I straighten things out and stop trying to play cupid?"

He studied her quietly. "You heard what was said out here, didn't you?"

She stared at the floor. "I got ears that hear pins falling. I was all excited about it, I thought you two were... Well, it's not my business to arrange people's lives, and I've only just realized it. I'll mind my own business from now on." She looked up. "She'll be all right, won't she? Thanks to us, she doesn't even have a job now."

He was dying inside, and that thought didn't help one bit. He didn't want her to go, but he was going to have to let her.

"She'll be all right," he said, for his own benefit as well as Lillian's. Of course she'd be all right. She was tough. And it was for the best. He didn't want to get married.

What if she went back and married someone else? His heart skipped a beat and he scowled.

"Can she come back, at least to visit?" Lillian asked sadly.

"Of course she can!" he grumbled. "She's your niece."

Lillian managed a smile. "Thanks for letting her come. You could have fired me."

"Not on your life—I'd starve to death." He smiled halfheartedly. "I'd better change."

A truck started up, and they both looked toward the window as Mari went past sitting beside Billy in the ranch truck.

Ward's face hardened. He turned on his heel without a word and went up the staircase. Lillian sighed, watching him. Well, the jig was up and no harm done. Or was there? He did look frustrated. She turned and went toward the kitchen. Maybe things might work out better than she had expected. She hummed a little, remembering the explosive force of that argument she'd overheard. And then she smiled. Where there was smoke, there was fire, her daddy used to say.

* * *

A week later, back in Atlanta, Mari was just getting over bouts of crying. Her small savings account was enough to pay the rent for the next month, thank goodness. She had bought groceries and cleaned her apartment and done her best not to think about what had happened in Texas.

Getting a job was the big problem, and she haunted the unemployment office for secretarial positions. There just weren't any available, but when there was an opening for a beginning bank clerk, she jumped at it. She hated figures and adding numbers, but it wasn't a good time to be choosy. She reported for work at a big bank in downtown Atlanta, and began the tedious process of learning to use computers and balance accounts.

After Mari was settled in Aunt Lillian called to make sure she'd made it home all right.

"I'm sorry, girl," the older woman said gruffly. "I never meant to cause you any hurt. I just wanted someone to look after you when I was gone. Now that I know I'm going to live, of course, I can do it by myself."

Mari was touched by her aunt's concern, even though she felt as if part of her had died. "I'll be okay," Mari promised brightly. "I'm sorry I had to leave so suddenly. I guess you figured out that we'd had a big argument."

"Hard to miss, the way you were going at each other before you left," Lillian said. "I knew the jig was up when he asked if you had the bus fare. He said you both knew I'd been spinning tales."

"We knew almost from the beginning," Mari said with a sigh. "We played along because we both think so much of you. But no more cupid, all right? You're much too tall to pass for the little guy, and you'd look pretty funny in a diaper carrying a bow and arrow."

Lillian actually laughed. "Guess I would, at that." She paused. "The boss left an hour ago for Hawaii. He said it was business, but he wasn't carrying any briefcase. He looked pretty torn up."

That would have been encouraging if Mari hadn't known him so well, but she didn't allow herself to feel hopeful. She wanted to tell Lillian just what the scalawag had offered to do, but she didn't want to crush all her aunt's illusions. He had been pretty good to Lillian, after all. He could afford to be. It was only eligible women he seemed to have it in for.

"He'll be back in form in no time," Mari told her aunt. "He'll proabably find some new woman to make passes at in Hawaii."

"He made a pass?" Lillian sounded almost girlish with glee.

Mari groaned, realizing what she'd given away. "Well, that was what you wanted, wasn't it?" she asked miserably. "You got your wish, but it wasn't commitment he had in mind."

"No man in his right mind ever wants to make a commitment," the other woman assured her. "They have to be led into it."

"I don't want to lead your boss anywhere except maybe into quicksand," Mari said darkly.

"You will come and see me again, won't you?" Lillian probed gently. "When you get over being mad at him?"

"Someday maybe."

"How about a job? Do you have any prospects yet?"

"Finally," Mari sighed. "I started working in the accounts department of a bank this morning."

"Good girl. I knew you'd bounce back quickly. I love you, Marianne."

Mari smiled in spite of herself. "I love you, too, Aunt Lillian. Take care of yourself. Please take your pills."

"I will, I promise. Good night."

Mari hung up and stared at the receiver. So the boss had gone to Hawaii. How nice for him. Balmy breezes, blooming flowers, beautiful women doing the hula. Well, he wouldn't be depressed for long or even missing the one that got away. Thank goodness she'd had sense enough to refuse his proposition. At least she still had her pride and her self-respect.

"And they'll keep you very warm on winter nights, too," Mari muttered to herself before she went to bed.

The bank job was interesting, at least, and she met some nice people. She liked Lindy and Marge, with whom she worked, and there was even a nice young assistant vice president named Larry, who was single and redheaded and just plain nice. She began to have coffee and sweet rolls with him in the mornings the second week she was at the bank. Little by little she was learning to live without the shadow of Ward Jessup.

Or she told herself she was. But the memory of him haunted her. She could close her eyes and feel the warm, hard crush of his mouth, the tantalizing seduction of his big hands. It had been so beautiful between them, so special. At no time in her life had she felt more secure or safe than she had with him. Despite his faults he was more man than she'd ever known. She found that love forgave a lot. She missed him terribly. Sometimes just seeing the back of a dark-headed tall man would be enough to make her heart jump. Or if she heard a deep masculine voice. Or if she saw Texas license plates on a car. She began to wonder if she was going to survive being away from him.

She called Lillian the third week, just to see how her aunt was getting along, she told herself. But it wasn't Lillian who answered the phone.

When she heard Ward's deep voice, her heart ran away. She hadn't realized how shattering it was going to be to talk to him. She'd assumed Lillian would answer.

"Hello?" he repeated impatiently.

Mari took a calming breath. "Is Aunt Lillian there, please?" she asked formally.

There was a long pause. She couldn't know that hearing her voice had made a similar impact on him.

"Hello, Mari," he said quietly. "Are you all right?"

"I'm very well, thank you. How is Aunt Lillian?"

"She's fine. It's her church social night. Billy ran her over there in the pickup. She'll be home around nine, I guess. Have you got a job?"

That was no business of his, especially seeing as how he'd caused her to lose the one she had in the first place. But hearing his voice had done something to her pride.

"Yes, I'm working at a bank," she told him, mentioning its name. "It's big and convenient to where I live. I work with nice people, and I'm making a better salary there than at the garage. You needn't worry about me."

"But I do," he said quietly. "I worry about you a lot. And I miss you," he added curtly, the words so harsh that they sounded quite involuntary.

She closed her eyes, gripping the receiver. "Do you?" she asked unsteadily, trying to laugh. "I can't imagine that."

"Someday soon I may work on making you imagine it," he said, his voice deep and slow and sensuous.

"I thought I'd told you already that I am not in the market for a big bank account and my own luxury apartment in Victoria, Texas," she returned, hating the unsteadiness that would tell him how much that hateful proposition had hurt her.

He said something rough under his breath. "Yes, I know that," he said gruffly. "I wish you were here. I wish we could talk. I made the biggest mistake of my life with you, Marianne. But I think it might help if you understood why."

Mistake. So now that was all he felt about those magical times they'd had. It had all been just a mistake. And he was sorry.

Tears burned her eyes, but she kept her voice steady. "There's no need to explain," she said gently. "I understand already. You told me how much you loved your freedom."

"It wasn't altogether just that," he returned. "You said Lillian had told you about what happened to me, about the woman I planned to marry."

"Yes."

He sighed heavily. "I suppose she and my mother colored my opinion of women more than I'd realized. I've seen women as nothing more than gold-digging opportunists for most of my adult life. I've used them that way. Anything physical came under the heading of permissible pleasure with me, and I paid for it like I paid for business deals. But until you came along, I never had a conscience. You got under my skin, honey. You're still there."

She imagined that he hadn't told anyone what he was telling her. And while it was flattering, it was disturbing, too. He was explaining why he'd made that "mistake" and was trying to get them back on a friendly footing. She remembered him saying the night he'd come to her room that he'd had that intention even then. It was like lighting a match to the paper of her hopes. An ending.

"Don't let me wear on your conscience, Ward," she said quietly. "You can't help the way you are. I'm a puritan. An old-fashioned prude. I won't change, either, even if the whole world does. So I guess I'll be like Aunt Lillian when I'm her age. Going to church socials and playing cupid for other women..." Her voice broke. "Listen, I have to go."

"No," he ground out. "Marianne, listen to me!"

"Goodbye, Ward."

She hung up before he could hear the tears that were falling hotly down her cheeks, before the break in her voice got worse. She went to bed without calling back. He'd tell Lillian she'd called, she knew, but she couldn't bear the risk that he might answer the phone again. Her heart was in tatters.

She went to work the next morning with her face still pale and her eyes bloodshot from the night before. She sat at her desk mechanically, answering the phone, going over new accounts, smiling at customers. Doing all the right things. But her mind was still on Ward and the sound of his voice and the memory of him that was eating her alive.

It would get better, wouldn't it? It had to! She couldn't go on like this, being haunted by a living ghost, so much in love that she could barely function as a human being. She'd never understood the idea of a couple being halves of the same whole until she met Ward. Now it made perfect sense because she felt as if part of her was missing.

When a long shadow fell across her desk just before lunchtime, she didn't even look up.

"I'll be with you in just a minute," she said with a forced smile as she finished listing a new account. And then she looked up and her body froze.

Ward stared down at her like a blind artist who could suddenly see again. His green eyes found every shadow, every line, every curve of her face in the stark, helpless silence that followed. Around them was the buzz of distant voices, the tap of fingers on keyboards, the ringing of telephones. And closer there was the rasp of Mari's hurried breathing, the thump of her heart shaking the silky pink blouse she was wearing with her gray skirt.

Ward was wearing a suit—a very elegant three-piece beige one that made him look even taller than he actually was. He had a creamy dress Stetson in one big hand, and his face looked thinner and drawn. His green eyes were as bloodshot as hers, as if he hadn't slept well. She thought as she studied him that he was the handsomest man she'd ever seen. If only he wasn't such a cold-blooded snake.

She stiffened defensively, remembering their last meeting. "Yes, sir?" she said with cold politeness. "May I help you?"

"Cut that out," he muttered. "I've had a long flight and no breakfast, and I feel like hell."

"I would like to point out that I work here," she informed him. "I have no time to socialize with old acquaintances. If you want to open an account, I'll be delighted to assist you. That's what I do here. I open accounts."

"I don't want to open an account," he said through his teeth.

"Then what do you want?" she asked.

"I came to take you home—where you belong." He searched her puzzled eyes. "Your boss will be sorry you have to leave, but he'll understand. You can come with me right now."

She blinked. Somewhere along the line she was sure that she'd missed something.

"I can what?" she asked.

"Come with me right now," he repeated. He turned the Stetson in his hands. "Don't you remember my condition? I'm dying, remember. I have something vaguely terminal, although medical science will triumph in plenty of time to save me."

"Huh?" she said blankly. None of this was getting through to her. She just stared at him.

"You're going to help me write my memoirs, remember?" he persisted.

"You aren't dying!" she burst out, coming to her senses at last.

"Shhhhh!" he said curtly, glancing stealthily around. "Somebody might hear you!"

"I can't quit! I just started working here the week before last!"

"You have to quit," he insisted. "If I go home without you, Lillian is going to starve me to death. She's getting her revenge in the kitchen. Small portions. Desserts without sugar. Diet foods." He shuddered. "I'm a shadow of my former self."

She glared at him. "Poor old thing," she said with poisonous sweetness.

He glared back. "I am not old. I'm just hitting my prime."

"That's nothing to do with me," she assured him. "I hope you didn't come all the way to Atlanta just to make this little scene!"

"I came to take you back with me," he replied. His eyes took on a determined hardness. "And, by God, I'm taking you back. If I have to pick you up bodily and carry you out of here in a fireman's lift."

Her heart jumped, but she didn't let him see how he was disturbing her. "I'll scream my head off," she said shortly.

"Good. Then everyone will think you're in pain, and I'll tell them I'm taking you to the hospital for emergency treatment." He glared at her. "Well?"

He had a stubborn streak that even outmatched her own. She weighed the possibilities. If he carried her out by force, she'd lose all credibility with her colleagues. If she fought him in front of everyone, Ward would get all the sympathy, and Mari would look like a heartless shrew. He had her over a barrel.

"Why?" she asked, her voice quiet and defeated. "Why not just let me stay here?"

He searched her eyes. "Your aunt misses you," he said gruffly.

"She could call me collect and talk to me," she replied. "There's no reason at all for me to go back to Texas and complicate my life and yours."

"My life is pretty boring right now, if you want to know the truth." He sighed, watching her. "I don't even enjoy foreclosing on people anymore. Besides all that, my cousin Bud's come to stay, and he's driving me out of my mind."

Cousin Bud was a familiar name. He was the one Ward's fiancée had wound up marrying for a brief time.

She couldn't imagine Ward actually welcoming the man as a guest.

"I'm surprised that you let him," she confessed.

He stared at her. "So you know all about that, too?"

She flushed, dropping her eyes to the desk. "Aunt Lillian mentioned it."

He sighed heavily. "Well, he's family. My grandmother worships him. I couldn't say no without having her jump all over me—and maybe even rush home to defend him. She's having a good time at Belinda's. No reason to disturb her."

She knew about old Mrs. Jessup as well, and she almost smiled at his lack of enthusiasm for his grandmother's company.

"If you've already got one houseguest, you surely don't need another one."

He shrugged. "There's plenty of room. My secretary quit," he added, studying his hat. "I sure could use some help in the office. You could almost name your own salary."

"You forced me to leave Texas in the first place," she shot back, glaring up at him. "You did everything but put me on the bus! You propositioned me!"

His cheeks had a sudden flush, and he looked away. "You can't actually like this job," he said shortly. "You said you hated working with numbers."

"I like eating," she replied. "It's hard to eat when you aren't making money."

"You could come home with me and make money," he said. "You could live with your aunt and help me keep Cousin Bud from selling off cattle under my nose."

"Selling off cattle?"

His powerful shoulders rose and fell. "He owns ten percent of the ranch. I had a weak moment when he was eighteen and made him a graduation present of it. The thing is, I never know which ten percent he happens to be claiming at the moment. It seems to change quarterly." He brushed at a speck of dust on his hat. "Right now, he's sneaking around getting statistics on my purebred Santa Gertrudis bull."

"What could I do about Cousin Bud—*if* I went with you?" she asked reasonably.

"You could help me distract him," he said. "With you in the office, he couldn't very well get to any statistics. He couldn't find out where I keep that bull unless he found it on the computer. And you'd be watching the computer."

It was just an excuse, and she knew it. For reasons of his own it suited him to have her at the ranch. She didn't flatter herself that it was out of any abiding love. He probably did still want her, but perhaps it was more a case of wanting to appease Lillian. She frowned, thinking.

"Is my aunt all right?" she asked.

He nodded. "She's fine. I wouldn't lie to you about that. But she's lonesome. She hasn't been the same since you left." Neither had he, he thought, but he couldn't tell her. Not yet. She didn't trust him at all, and he couldn't really blame her.

She fiddled with a pencil, considering Ward's offer. She could tell him to go away and he would. And she'd never see him again. She could go on alone and take up the threads of her life. What a life it would be. What a long, lonely life.

"Come with me, Mari," he said softly. "This is no place for you."

She didn't look up. "I meant what I said before I left. If I come back, I don't...I don't want you to...to..."

He sighed gently. "I know, I know. You don't have to worry," he told her. "I won't proposition you. You have my word on that."

She shifted. "Then I'll go."

He forced back a smile. "Come on, then. I've got the tickets already."

She lifted her eyebrows. "Were you that confident?"

"Not confident at all," he replied. "But I figured I could always put my Stetson in one of the seats if you refused."

She did smile faintly at that. "I always heard that a real Texan puts his hat on the floor and his boots on the hat rack."

He lifted a tooled leather boot and studied it. "Yep," he said. "I guess I'd put my boots in the extra seat, at that. But I'd rather have you in it."

She got to her feet and put her work aside. "I need to see Mr. Blake, my boss."

"I'll wait." He wasn't budging.

After Mari had apologetically informed her boss of her departure, she picked up her purse, waved at her new friends and went quietly out the door with Ward. It felt odd, and she knew it was foolhardy. But she was too vulnerable still to refuse him. She only hoped that she could keep him from knowing just how vulnerable she was.

He drove her back to her apartment and then wandered around the living room while she packed.

His fingers brushed the spines of the thick volumes in her small bookcase. *"The Tudors of England,"* he murmured, "ancient Greece, Herodotus, Thucydides—quite a collection of history."

"I like history," she commented. "It's interesting reading about how other people lived in other times."

"Yes, I think so, too," he agreed. "I prefer Western history myself. I have a good collection of information on the Comanche and the cowboy period in south Texas, from the Civil War up to the 1880s."

She took her bag into the living room, watching the way he filled the room. He was so big. So masculine. He seemed to dwarf everything.

"We don't really know a lot about each other, do we?" he asked as she joined him. He turned, hands in his pockets, spreading the fabric of his trousers close against the powerful muscles of his legs.

"Getting to know women isn't one of your particular interests, from what I've heard," she returned quietly. "At least, not in any intellectual way."

"I explained why," he reminded her, and his green eyes searched her blue ones. "It isn't easy learning to trust people."

She nodded. "I suppose not." She wanted to ask him why he seemed to be so interested in where she lived, but she was too shy. "I'm packed."

He glanced toward her suitcase. "Enough for a little while?"

"Enough for a week or so," she said. "You didn't say how long I was to stay."

He sighed heavily. "That's something we'll leave for later. Right now I just want to go home." He looked around him. "It's like you," he said finally. "Bright. Cheerful, Very homey."

She hadn't felt bright and cheerful and homey in recent weeks. She'd felt depressed and miserable. But it fascinated her that her apartment told him so much.

"It doesn't have an indoor stream," she commented.

He smiled slowly. "No, it doesn't. Good thing. With my batting average so far, I guess I'd be in it by now, wouldn't I?"

She cleared her throat, feeling embarrassed. "I didn't mean to push you in the river."

"Didn't you? It seemed like it at the time." He searched her eyes quietly. "I meant what I said, Marianne. I won't make any more insulting propositions."

"I appreciate that. I'm just sorry that I gave you such a poor opinion of me," she added, admitting her own guilt. "I shouldn't have let things go on the way they did."

He moved closer, lifting his hands to her shoulders, lightly holding her in front of him. "What we did together was pretty special," he said hesitantly. "I couldn't have stopped it any more than you could. Let's try not to look back. That part of our relationship is over."

He sounded final, and she felt oddly hurt. She stared at his vest, watching the slow rise and fall of his chest.

"Yes," she murmured.

He looked down at her silky dark hair, smelled the soft floral scent that clung to her, and his heart began to throb. It had been so long since he'd held her, kissed her. He wanted to, desperately, but he'd just tied his own hands by promising not to start anything.

"Do you like kittens?" he asked unexpectedly.

Her eyes came up, brightly blue and interested. "Yes. Why?"

"We've got some," he said with a grin. "Lillian found an old mama cat squalling at the back door in a driving rain and couldn't help herself. The very next morning we had four little white kittens with eyes as blue as—" he searched hers with a disturbing intensity "—as yours."

"You let her keep the kittens?" she asked softly.

He shifted restlessly. "Well, it was raining," he muttered. "The poor little things would have drowned if I'd put them outside."

She wasn't buying that. Odd, how well she'd come to know him in the little time she'd spent on his ranch. "And . . . ?" she prodded with raised eyebrows.

He almost smiled at the knowing look on her face. She knew him, warts and all, all right. "Cousin Bud's got one hell of an allergy to little kitties."

He was incorrigible. She burst out laughing. "Oh, you black-hearted fiend, you!" she groaned.

"I like little kitties," he said with mock indignation. "If he doesn't, he can leave, can't he? I mean, I don't lock him in at night or anything."

If love was knowing all about someone—the good things and the bad—and loving them just the same, then it sure did apply here, she mused silently. "Ward Jessup," she said, sighing, "you just won't leave Bud alone, will you?"

"Sure I will, if he'll go home and leave my bull alone," he returned. "My God, you don't know how hard I fought to get that critter into my breeding program. I outbid two of the richest Texans in cattle to get him!"

"And now Cousin Bud wants him. What for?" she asked.

"Beats me." He sighed. "Probably for his advertising agency."

She sat down on the sofa. "He wants your bull for an ad agency?" she asked dubiously.

His eyebrows rose while his brain began to grasp what she was thinking. "Ad agency...oh, no, hell, no, he isn't going to use the bull to pose for male underwear commercials! He wants to sell it to finance expanding his advertising agency!"

"Well, don't glare at me, it sounded like he wanted to make a male model out of it," she defended herself.

He sighed heavily. "Woman, you're going to be my undoing," he said. And probably she would if he let himself think too hard about just why he'd come all this way after her. But missing her was just part of the torturous process. Now he had to prove to himself that he could have her around and not go off his head anymore. He still wanted her for certain, but marriage wouldn't suit him any more than being his mistress would suit her. So they'd be...friends. Sure. Friends. Lillian would stop starving him. There. He had noble motives. He just had to get them cemented in his mind, that was all.

"Can't you just tell Cousin Bud to go home?" she asked curiously.

"I have!" he grumbled. "Lillian has, too. But every time we get him to the front door, he calls up my grandmother and she raises hell with Lillian and me for not offering him our hospitality."

"She must like him a lot," she mused.

"More than she likes me, I'm afraid," he returned. He whirled his Stetson in his hands. "I'll give you one of the kittens if you want it."

"Bribery," she said in a stage whisper and actually grinned.

He grinned back. She was pretty that way. "Sure it is," he said shamelessly. He glanced around her small apartment. "Will they let you keep a cat here?"

"I guess so. I haven't ever asked." So he was already planning for her to come back here, she thought miserably.

He shrugged. "You might not want to come back here, though," he said unexpectedly. He smiled slowly. "You might like working for me. I'm a good boss. You can have every Sunday off, and I'll only keep you at the computer until nine every night."

"You old slave driver!"

He didn't laugh as she'd expected him to. He just stared at her. "Am I old to you?" he asked softly as if it really mattered.

Watch it, girl, she warned herself. Take it easy, don't let the old devil fox you. "No," she said finally. "I don't think you're that old."

"To a kid like you I guess I seem that way," he persisted, searching her blue eyes with his darkening green ones.

She didn't like remembering how much older she felt because of his searching ardor. She dropped her eyes to the floor. "You said the past was over. That we'd forget it."

He shifted his booted feet. "I guess I did, honey," he agreed quietly. "Okay. If that's how you want it."

She looked up unexpectedly and found a strange, haunting look on his dark face. "It's an impasse, don't you think?" she asked him. "You don't want a wife, and I don't want an unattached temporary lover. So all that's really left is friendship."

He clutched the hat tighter. "You're making it sound cheap," he said in a faintly dangerous tone. He didn't like what she was saying.

"Isn't it?" she persisted, rising to her feet. He still towered over her, but it gave her a bit of an advantage. "You'd get all the benefits of married life with none of the responsibility. And what would I get, Ward? A little notoriety as the boss's mistress, and after you got tired of me, I'd be handed some expensive parting gift and left alone with my memories. No respectability, no self-respect, tons of guilt and loneliness. I think that's a pretty poor bargain."

"You little prude," he said curtly. "What do you know about grown-up problems, you with your spotless conscience? It's so easy, isn't it, all black and white. You tease a man with your body until he's crazy for it, you try to trap him into a marriage he doesn't want, you take whatever you can get and walk out the door. What does the man have out of all that?"

His attitude shocked her. She hadn't realized just how poisoned he was against the female sex until he made that bitter statement.

"Is that what she did to you?" she asked gently. "Did she tease you beyond endurance and then marry someone else because what you gave her wasn't enough?"

His face grew harder than she'd ever seen it. He'd never talked about it, but she was forcing his hand.

"Yes," he said curtly. "That's precisely what she did. And if I'd been fool enough to marry her, she'd have cut my throat emotionally and financially, and she wouldn't even have looked back to see if I was bleeding to death on her way to the bank!"

She moved closer to him, hating that hurt in his eyes, that disillusionment that had drawn his face muscles taut. "Shall I tell you what most women really want from marriage? They want the closeness of caring for one man all their lives. Looking after him, caring about him, doing little things for him, loving him . . . sharing good times and bad. A good marriage doesn't have a lot to do with money, from what I've seen. But mutual trust and caring about each other makes all the difference. Money can't buy those."

He felt himself weakening and hated it. She was under his skin, all right, and it was getting worse all the time. He wanted her until he ached, and it didn't stop with his body. She stirred him inside, in ways no other woman ever had. Except Caroline. Caroline. Would he ever forget?

"Pretty words," he said bitterly, searching her eyes.

"Pretty ideals," she corrected. "I still believe in those old virtues. And someday I'll find a man who believes in them, too."

"In some graveyard, maybe."

"You are so cynical!" she accused, exasperated.

"I had good teachers," he retorted, slamming his Stetson down on his head to cock it arrogantly over one eye. "Are you ready?"

"I'm ready," she muttered, sounding every bit as bad-tempered as he did.

He took her bag in one hand and opened the apartment door with the other. She followed him out, locked the door with a sigh and put the key in her purse. Her life was so unpredictable these days. Just like the man beside her.

The commercial flight seemed longer than it actually was. Mari had found a few magazines to read at the huge Atlanta Hartsfield International Airport, and it was a good thing that she had because Ward pulled his hat over his eyes and folded his arms and he hadn't said one word to her yet. The flight attendants were already serving their lunch, but Ward only glanced up, refusing food. Mari knew, as she nibbled at ham and cheese on a bun, that he had to be furious or sick. He never refused food for any other reason.

Mari was sorry that they'd quarreled. She shouldn't have been because, if he was angry, at least he wouldn't be making passes at her. But if he stayed angry, it was going to make working for him all that much harder, and she'd promised, God knew why, to do his secretarial work. Now she couldn't imagine what had possessed her to agree. At the time it had seemed a wonderful idea. Of course, she'd had some crazy idea that he'd cared a little in order to come all that way to get her. Now it was beginning to seem as if he hated himself for the very thought. Mari was miserable. She should have said no. Then she remembered that she had, and that, ultimately, she had little choice in the matter.

She sighed over her food, glancing at him under the hat. "Aren't you hungry?" she offered.

"If I was hungry, I'd be eating, wouldn't I?" he muttered indistinctly.

She shrugged. "Then go right ahead and starve if you want to. I couldn't care less."

He lifted the brim of the hat and glared at her. "Like hell you couldn't," he retorted. "You and your pristine little conscience would sting for months."

"Not on your account," she assured him as she finished the ham. "After all, you're starving yourself. I haven't done anything."

"You've ruined my appetite," he said curtly.

Her eyebrows arched. "How did I do that, pray tell? By mentioning the word marriage? Some people don't mind getting married. I expect to do it myself one of these days. You see, I don't have your blighted outlook. I think you get out of a relationship what you put into it."

His green eyes narrowed, glittering. "And just what would you plan to put into one?"

"Love, laughter and a lot of pillow talk," she said without hesitation. "I expect to be everything my husband will ever want, in and out of bed. So you just go right ahead and have affairs, Mr. Jessup, until you're too old to be capable of it, and then you can live alone and count your money. I'll let my grandchildren come and visit you from time to time."

He seemed to swell all over with indignation. "I can get married any time I want to," he said shortly. "Women hound me to death to marry them!"

Her mouth made a soft whistle. "Do tell? And here you are pushing forty and still single . . ."

"I'm pushing thirty-six, not forty!"

"What's the difference?" she asked reasonably.

He opened his mouth to answer, glared fiercely at her and then jerked his hat down over his eyes with a muttered curse. He didn't speak to her again until the plane landed in Texas.

"Are you going to ignore me the rest of the way?" Mari said finally when they were in the Chrysler just a few minutes outside of Ravine.

"I can't carry on a civilized conversation without having you blow up at me," he said gruffly.

"I thought it was the other way around." She picked a piece of lint off her sleeve. "You're the one doing all the growling, not me. I just said that I wanted to get married and have babies.''

"Will you stop saying that?" He shifted angrily in the seat. "I'll get hives just thinking about it."

"I don't see why. They'll be my babies, not yours."

He was grinding his teeth together. He'd just realized something that he hadn't considered. Cousin Bud was young and personable and hungry to settle down. He'd take one look at this sweet innocent and be hanging by his heels, trying to marry her. Bud wasn't like Ward; he was carefree and his emotions were mostly on the surface. He didn't have scars from Caroline, and he wasn't afraid of love. In fact, he seemed to walk around in a perpetual state of it. And here was Ward, bringing him the perfect victim. The only woman Ward had ever wanted and hadn't got. Bud might be the one... Suddenly he slammed on the brakes.

"What!" Mari burst out, gasping as she grasped the dash. "What is it?"

"Just a rabbit," he muttered with a quick glance in her direction. "Sorry."

She stared at him. She hadn't seen any rabbit, and he sure was pale. What was wrong with him?

"Are you all right?" she asked cautiously, her voice soft with helpless concern.

It was the concern that got to him. He felt vulnerable with her. That evidence of her soft heart wound strands around him, binding him. He didn't want marriage or ties or babies! But when he looked at her, he felt such sweet longings, such exquisite pleasure. It had nothing to do with sex or carefree lust. It was... disturbing.

"Yes," he said quietly. "I'm all right."

A little farther down the road he suddenly pulled into a shallow farm road that was little more than ruts in the grass. It went beyond a closed fence, through a pasture, toward a distant grove of trees.

"My grandfather's place," he said as he turned off the engine. "My father was born out there, where you see those trees. It was a one-room shack in those days, and my grandmother once fought off a Comanche raiding party with an old Enfield rifle while my grandfather was up in Kansas on a trail drive."

He got out of the car and opened her door. "I know the owner," he said when she was standing beside him. "He doesn't mind if I come here. I like to see the old place sometimes."

He didn't ask if she wanted to. He just held out his big hand. Without hesitation she placed her slender one in it and felt tingly all over as his fingers closed warmly around it.

She felt small beside him as they walked. He opened and closed the gate, grinning at her curious stare.

"Any cattleman knows the value of a closed fence," he remarked as he grasped her hand once more and began to walk along the damp ruts. It had rained recently and there were still patches of mud. "In the old days a rancher might very well shoot a greenhorn who left a gate open and let his cattle get out."

"Were there really Indian raids around here?" she asked.

"Why, sure, honey," he said, smiling down at her. "Comanche, mostly, and there were Mexican bandidos who raided the area, too. Cattle rustling was big business back then. It still is in some areas. Except now they do it with big trucks, and in the old days they had to drive the herd out of the country or use a running iron."

She glanced up curiously. "What's a running iron?"

"A branding iron with a curved tip," he said. "It was used to alter brands so a man could claim another man's cattle. Here." He let go of her hand and found a stick and drew a couple of brands in the dirt, explaining how a running iron could be used to add an extra line or curve to an existing brand and change its shape entirely.

"That's fascinating!" she said.

"It's also illegal, but it happened quite a lot." He put the stick down and stuck his hands in his pockets, smiling as he looked around at feathery mesquite and live oak trees and open pasture. "God, it's pretty here," he said. "Peaceful, rustic... I never get tired of the land. I guess it's that damned Irish in my ancestry." He glanced down. "My grandmother, now, says it's British. But just between us, I don't think O'Mara is a British name, and that was my great-grandmother's maiden name."

"Maybe your grandmother doesn't like the Irish," she suggested.

"Probably not since she was jilted by a dashing Irishman in the war."

"Which war?" Mari asked cautiously.

"I'm afraid to ask," he said conspiratorially. "I'm not quite sure just how old she is. Nobody knows."

"How exciting," she said with a laugh.

He watched her with a faint smile, fascinated by the change in her when she was with him. That pale, quiet woman in the bank bore no resemblance to this bright, beautiful one. He scowled, watching her wander through the wooded area where the old ramshackle ranch house sagged under the weight of age and rotting timbers and rusting tin. She made everything new and exciting, and the way she seemed to light up when he was near puzzled him, excited him. He wondered if she might care about him. Love him . . .

She whirled suddenly, her face illuminated with surprised delight. "Ward, look!"

There were pink roses by the steps. A profusion of vines bore pink roses in tight little clusters, and their perfume was everywhere.

"Aren't they beautiful!" she enthused, bending to smell them. "What a heavenly aroma!"

"Legend has it that my father's grandmother, Mrs. O'Mara, brought those very roses from Calhoun County, Georgia, and nursed them like babies until they took hold here. She carried them across the frontier in a pot. In a Conestoga wagon, and saved them from fire, flood, swollen river crossings, robbers, Indians and curious little children. And they're still here. Like the land," he mused, staring around with eyes full of pride. "The land will be here longer than any of us and very little changed despite our meddling."

She smiled. "You sound just like a rancher."

He turned. "I am a rancher."

"Not an oilman?"

He shrugged. "I used to think oil was the most important thing in the world. Until I got plenty of it. Now I don't know what's the most important thing anymore. My whole life seems to be upside down lately." He stared straight at her. "I was a happy man until you came along."

"You were a vegetable until I came along," she replied matter-of-factly. "You thought robbing people was all right."

"Why, you little devil," he said in a husky undertone, and his eyes went a glittering green. "You little devil!"

She laughed because there was as much mischief as threat in that look. She started running across the meadow, a picture in her full gray skirt and pretty pink blouse, with her dark hair gleaming in the sun. He ran after her in time to catch the colorful glimmer of something moving just in front of her in the grass.

"Mari!" he called out, his voice deep and cutting and full of authority. "Stop!"

She did, with one foot in midair, because he sounded so final. She didn't look down. With her inborn terror of snakes, she knew instinctively what he was warning her about.

"Don't move, baby," he breathed, stopping himself just within reach of a fallen limb from one of the oaks. "Don't move, don't breathe. It's all right. Just stand perfectly still...."

He moved with lightning speed picking up a heavy branch and swinging his arm down, slamming. There was a feverish rattling, like bacon sizzling in a pan, and then only a bloody, writhing, coiling mass on the ground.

She was numb with unexpressed terror, her eyes huge at the thing on the ground that, only seconds ago, could have taken her life. She started to speak, to tell him how grateful she was, when he caught her up in his arms and brought his hard mouth down bruisingly on hers.

She couldn't breathe, couldn't move. He was hurting her, and she hardly noticed. His mouth was telling her things words couldn't. That he was afraid for her, that he was glad she was safe, that he'd take care of her. She let him tell her that way, glad of his strength. Her arms curled around his broad shoulders, and she sighed under his warm, hungry mouth, savoring its rough ardor.

"My God," he whispered unsteadily, his mouth poised over hers, his eyes dark in a face that was pale under its tan, his breath rough. "My God, one more step and it would have had you!"

"I'm all right, thanks to you." She managed to smile through the shaking relief, her fingers traced his rough cheek, his mouth. "Thank you."

He lifted her against his body, as rugged as any frontier man would have been, his face mirroring pride and masculinity. "Thank me, then," he whispered, opening his mouth as he bent to her lips. "Thank me..."

She did, so hungrily that he had to put her away from him or let her feel how easily she could arouse him. He held her by the waist, breathing unsteadily, watching her flushed face.

"We agreed that wouldn't happen again," he said.

She nodded, searching his eyes.

"But the circumstances were... unusual," he continued.

"Yes," she whispered, her eyes falling to his hard mouth with languorous remembered pleasure. "Unusual."

"Stop looking at me like that, or it won't end with kisses," he threatened huskily. "You felt what you were doing to me."

She averted her eyes and moved away. Sometimes she forgot how experienced he was until he made a remark like that and emphasized it. She had to remember that she was just another woman. He felt responsible for her, that was why he'd reacted like that to the snake. It wasn't anything personal.

"Well, thanks for saving me," she said, folding her arms over her breasts as she walked back to the car, and carefully she avoided looking at the dead snake as she went.

"Watch where you put your feet, will you?" he asked from behind her. "One scare like that is enough."

Scare for which one of us? she wanted to ask. But she was too drained to say it. Her mouth ached for his. She could hardly bear to remember that she'd inflicted this torment on herself by letting him bring her out here. How was she going to bear days or weeks of it, of being near him and being vulnerable and having no hope at all for a future that included him?

Chapter Ten

Ward was quiet the rest of the way to the ranch, but he kept watching Mari and the way he did it was exciting. Once he reached across the space between them and found her hand. He kept it close in his until traffic in Ravine forced him to let go, and Mari found her heart doing spins.

She didn't know how to handle this new approach. She couldn't quite trust him yet, and she wasn't altogether sure that he didn't have some ulterior motive for bringing her back. After all, he wasn't hampered by emotions as she was.

Lillian came quickly out to meet them, looking healthy and fit and with a healed leg.

"Look here," she called to Mari and danced a jig. "How's that for an improvement?" She laughed gaily.

"Terrific!" Mari agreed. She ran forward to embrace the older woman warmly. "It's good to see you again."

"He's been horrible," Lillian whispered while Ward was getting the bag out of the car. "Just horrible. He moped around for days after you left and wouldn't eat at all."

"He should have foreclosed on somebody, then," Mari said matter-of-factly. "That would have cheered him up."

Lillian literally cackled. "Shame on you," she said with a laugh.

"What's all the humor about?" Ward asked as he joined them, his expression tight and mocking.

"Your appetite," Mari volunteered tongue in cheek.

Lillian had turned to go back inside. Ward leaned down, holding Mari's eyes. "You know more about that than most women do, honey," he said in a seductive undertone. "And if you aren't careful, you may learn even more."

"Don't hold your breath," she told him, rushing away before she fell under the spell of his mocking ardor.

"Where's Bud?" Ward asked as they entered the hall.

"Did somebody call me?" came a laughing voice from the study.

The young man who came out to greet them was a total surprise for Mari. She'd been expecting Ward's cousin to be near his own age, but Bud was much younger. He was in his late twenties, at a guess, and lithe and lean and handsome. He had Ward's swarthy complexion, but his eyes were brown instead of green and his hair was lighter than his cousin's. He was a striking man, especially in the leather and denim he was wearing.

"Have you been sneaking around after my bull again?" Ward demanded.

"Now, Cousin," Bud said soothingly, "how would I find him in there?" He jerked his hand toward the study and shuddered. "It would take a team of secretaries a week just to find the desk!"

"Speaking of secretaries," Ward said, "this is my new one. Marianne Raymond, this is Bud Jessup. My cousin."

"Ah, the much-talked-about niece," Bud murmured, winking at Mari. "Hello, Georgia peach. You sure do your home state proud."

Ward didn't like Bud's flirting. His eyes told his cousin so, which only made Bud more determined than ever.

"Thank you," Mari was saying, all smiles. "It's nice to meet you at last."

"Same here," Bud said warmly, moving forward.

"Here, son," Ward said, tossing the bag at him. "You can put that in the guest room, if you don't mind. I'm sure Mari would like to see the study." Before anybody could say anything else, Ward had taken Mari by the arm and propelled her none too gently into the study.

He slammed the door behind them, bristling with masculine pride, and turned to glare at her. "He's not marrying material," he told her immediately, "so don't take him too seriously. He just likes to flirt."

"Maybe I do, too," she began hotly.

He shook his head, moving slowly toward her. "Not you, honey," he replied. "You aren't the flirting kind. You're no butterfly. You're a little house wren, all feathered indignation and quick eyes and nesting instinct."

"You think you know a lot about me, don't you?" She faltered on the last word because she was backing away from him and almost fell over a chair. He kept coming, looming over her with threatening eyes and sheer size.

"I know more than I ever expected to," he agreed, coming closer. "Stop running. We both know it's me you really want, not Bud."

She drew herself up, glaring at him. "You conceited..."

He moved quickly, scooping her up in his arms, holding her off the floor, his eyes wavering between amusement and ardor. "Go ahead, finish it," he taunted.

She could have if he hadn't been so close. His breath was minty and it brushed her lips when he breathed, warm and moist. He made her feel feminine and vulnerable, and when she looked at his hard mouth, she wanted to kiss it.

"Your office," she swallowed, "is a mess."

"So am I," he whispered huskily, searching her eyes. "So is my life. Oh, God, I missed you!"

That confession was her undoing. She looked up at him and couldn't look away, and her heart felt like a runaway engine. Her head fell back onto his shoulder, and she watched him lower his dark head.

"Open your mouth when I put mine over it," he breathed against her lips. "Taste me..."

Her breath caught. She was reaching up, she could already feel the first tentative brushing of his warm lips when a knock at the door made them both jump.

He lifted his head with a jerky motion. "What is it?" he growled.

Mari trembling in his arms, heard a male voice reply, "Lillian's got coffee and cake in the dining room,

Cousin! Why don't you come and have some refreshment?''

"I'd like to have him, fricasseed," Ward muttered under his breath as Bud's laughing voice became dimmer along with his footsteps.

"I'd like some coffee," she said hesitantly even though she was still shaking with frustrated reaction and her voice wobbled.

He looked down into her eyes. "No, you wouldn't," he said huskily. "You'd like me. And I'd like you, right there on that long sofa where we almost made love the first time. And if it hadn't been for my meddling, jealous cousin, that's where we'd be right now!"

He put her down abruptly and moved away. "Come on, we'll have coffee." He stopped at the door with his hand on the knob. "For now," he added softly. "But one day, Marianne, we'll have each other. Because one day neither one of us is going to be able to stop."

She couldn't look at him. She couldn't even manage a defiant stare. It was the truth. She'd been crazy to come here, but there was no one to blame but herself.

From that first meeting, Cousin Bud seemed determined to drive Ward absolutely crazy. He didn't leave Mari alone with the older man for a second if he could help it. He found excuse after excuse to come into the office when she was typing things for Ward, and if she ever had to find Ward to ask a question, Bud would find them before they said two words to each other. Mari wondered if it might just be mischief on Bud's part, but Ward treated the situation as if he had a rival.

That in itself was amazing. Ward seemed possessive now, frankly covetous whenever Mari was near him. He shared things with her. Things about the ranch, about his plans for it, the hard work that had gone into its success. When he came home late in the evening, it was to Mari that he went, seeking her out wherever she might be, to ask for coffee or a sandwich or a slice of cake. Lillian took this new attitude with open delight, glad to have her former position usurped when she saw the way he was looking at her puzzled niece.

Bud usually managed to weasel in, of course, but there eventually came a night when he had business out of town. Ward came in about eight o'clock, covered in dust and half starved.

"I sure could use a couple of sandwiches, honey," he told Mari gently, pausing in the living room doorway. Lillian had gone to bed, and curled up on the sofa in her jeans and a yellow tank top, Mari was watching the credits roll after an entertainment special.

"Of course," she said eagerly and got up without bothering to look for her shoes.

He was even taller when she was barefoot, and he seemed amused by her lack of footwear.

"You look like a country girl," he remarked as she passed close by him, feeling the warmth of his big body.

"I feel like a country girl," she said with a pert smile. "Come on, big man, I'll feed you."

"How about some coffee to go with it?" he added as he followed her down the hall into the spacious kitchen.

"Easier done than said," she told him. She flicked the on switch of the small coffee machine, grinning at him when it started to perk. "I had it fixed and ready to start."

"Reading my mind already?" he teased. He pulled out a chair and sat down, sprawling with a huge stretch before he put his long legs out and rested his booted feet in another chair. "The days are getting longer, or I'm getting older," he said with a yawn. "I guess if I keep up this pace, before long you'll be pushing me around in a wheelchair.''

"Not you," she said with loving amusement. "You're not the type to give up and get old before your time. You'll still be chasing women when you're eighty-five.''

He sobered with amazing rapidity, his green eyes narrowing in his handsome face as he studied her graceful movements around the kitchen. "Suppose I told you that you're the only woman I'll want to chase when I'm eighty-five, Marianne?" he asked gently.

Her heart leaped, but she wasn't giving in to it that easily. He'd already come too close once and hurt her. She'd been deliberately keeping things light since she'd come back to the ranch, and she wasn't going to be trapped now.

She laughed. "Oh, I guess I'd be flattered.''

"Only flattered?" he mused.

She finished making the sandwiches and put them down on the table. "By that time I expect to be a grandmother many times over," she informed him as she went back to pour the coffee. "And I think my husband might object.''

He didn't like thinking about Marianne with a husband. His face darkened. He turned his attention to the sandwiches and began to eat.

"I have to go over to Ty Wade's place tomorrow," he murmured. "Want to come and meet Erin and the babies?''

She caught her breath. "Me? But won't I be in the way if you're going to talk business?''

He shook his head, holding her soft blue eyes. "You'll never be in my way, sweetheart," he said with something very much like tenderness in his deep voice. "Not ever.''

She smiled at him. The way he was looking at her made her feel trembly all over. He was weaving subtle webs around her, but without the wild passion he'd shown her at the beginning of their turbulent relationship. This was new and different. While part of her was afraid to trust it, another part was hungry for it and for him.

"How about it?" he asked, forcing himself to go slow, not to rush her. He'd already had to face the fact that he wasn't going to be able to let her go. Now it was a question of making her see that he didn't have ulterior motives, and she was as hard to trust as he was.

"I'd like to meet Mrs. Wade," she said after a minute. "She sounds like quite a lady."

He laughed under his breath. "If you'd known Ty before she came along, you'd think she was quite a lady," he agreed with a grin. "It took one special woman to calm down that cougar. You'll see what I mean tomorrow."

The next afternoon Mari climbed into the Chrysler beside Ward for the trip over to the Wades' place. Ward was wearing slacks with a striped, open-necked green shirt, and she had on a pretty green pantsuit with a gaily striped sleeveless blouse. He'd grinned when he noticed that their stripes matched.

Erin Wade opened the door, a picture in a gaily flowing lavender caftan. She looked as if she smiled a lot, and she was obviously a beauty when she was made up, with her long black hair and pretty green eyes. But she wasn't wearing makeup. She looked like a country girl, clean and fresh.

"Hello!" she said enthusiastically. "I'm glad you brought her, Ward. Hello, I'm Erin, and you have to be Marianne. Come in and see my boys!"

"I'm glad to meet you, too." Marianne grinned. "I've heard legends about you already."

"Have you, really?" Erin laughed. She was beautiful even without makeup, Marianne thought, the kind of beauty that comes from deep within and makes even homely women bright and lovely when it shows. "Well, Ty and I got off to a bad start, but we've come a long way in very little time. I don't think he has many regrets about getting married. Not even with twin boys."

"I can just see him now, changing a diaper." Ward chuckled.

Erin's green eyes widened. "But you can," she said. "Follow me."

Sure enough, there he was, changing a diaper. It looked so touching, the big, tough rancher Marianne had met before bending over that tiny, smiling, kicking baby on the changing table in a bedroom decorated with teddy bear wallpaper and mobiles.

"Oh, hello, Jessup," he murmured, glancing over his shoulder as he put the last piece of adhesive in place around the baby's fat middle. "Matthew was wet, I was just changing him," he told Erin. He glanced toward a playpen, where another baby was standing on unsteady little fat legs with both chubby hands on the rail, biting delightedly on the plastic edging. "Jason's hungry, I think. He's been trying to eat the playpen for the past five minutes."

"He's teething," Erin said, leaning over to pick him up and cuddle him while he cooed and patted her shoulder and chanted, "Da, Da, Da, Da."

Ty grinned mockingly at his frowning wife. "She hates that," he told the guests. "Most babies say Mama first. Both of them call me instead of her."

"Don't gloat." Erin stuck her tongue out at him. "You just remember who got up with them last night and let you sleep."

He winked at her, with torrents of love pouring on her from his light eyes. Marianne glanced up at Ward and found him watching her with the oddest look on his face. His green eyes went slowly down to her flat stomach and back up again, and she blushed because she knew what he was thinking. *Exactly* what he was thinking. She could read it in the sudden flare of his eyes, in the set of his face. She went hot all over with the unexpected passion that boiled up so suddenly and had to turn away to get herself under control again.

"How about some coffee?" Erin asked them, handing Jason to his dad. "Ward, if you'll bring the playpen, the boys can come with us."

Ward, to his credit, tried to figure out how the device folded up, but he couldn't seem to fathom it. Ty chuckled. "Here, if Marianne will hold the boys, I'll do it."

"Surely!" She took them, cooing to them both, loving their little chubby smiling faces and the way they tried to feel every inch of her face and hair as she carried them into the living room.

"Oh, how sweet," she cooed, kissing fat cheeks and heads that had just a smattering of hair. The twins had light eyes like their father, but they were green.

"Thank God they both take after Erin and not me," Ty said with a sigh as he set up the playpen and took the boys from Marianne to put them back in.

"You're not that bad," Ward remarked, cocking his head. "I've seen uglier cactus plants, in fact."

Ty glared at him. "If you want that second damned lease, you'd better clean up your act, Jessup."

Ward grinned. "Can I help it if you go asking for insults?"

"Watch it," Ty muttered, turning back to help Erin with the coffee service.

The men talked business, and Marianne and Erin talked babies and clothes and fashion. It was the most enjoyable afternoon Marianne had spent in a long time and getting to cuddle the babies was a bonus. She was reluctant to leave.

"Ward, you'll have to bring her back to see me," Erin insisted. "I don't have much company, and I do love to talk clothes."

"I will," Ward promised. He shook hands with Ty, and they said their goodbyes. As they drove away, Ty had one lean arm around Erin, looking as if he were part of her.

"That marriage will outlast this ranch," she murmured, watching the landscape turn gray with a sudden shower. It seemed chilly in the car with that wetness beating on the hood and windshield. "They seem so happy."

"They are," he agreed. He glanced at her and slowly pulled the truck off onto one of the farm roads, pulling up under a huge live oak tree before cutting the engine. "Would you like to guess why I stopped?" he asked, his voice slow and tender as he looked at her. "Or do you know?"

Chapter Eleven

No, Marianne thought, she didn't really have to wonder why he'd parked the car. His face gave her the answer. So did the heavy, quick rise and fall of his chest under the green-striped shirt. He looked so handsome that she could hardly take her eyes off him, and the sheer arrogance in his narrowed eyes was intimidating.

But she wasn't sure she wanted a sweet interlude with him. Her defenses were weak enough already. Suppose he insisted? Could she resist him if she let herself fall in that heady trap?

"I don't think this is a good idea," she began as he unfastened his seat belt and then hers.

"Don't you?" he asked. "Even after the way you went scarlet when I stared at your waistline in the twins' room? You knew what I was thinking, Marianne," he whispered, reaching for her. "You knew."

He lifted her across him, finding her mouth even as he eased her down against his arm with her head at the window. Outside rain was streaming down the glass, making a quick tattoo on the hood and the roof, as driving as the passion that began to take over Mari's blood.

He bit at her soft lips, tender little nips that made her want him. His big hand smoothed over her blouse, under it, finding the softness of her breast in its silky casing.

"Lie still," he whispered when her body jerked under that gentle probing. "It's been a long time since we've enjoyed each other like this. Too long."

He kissed her wide eyes shut and found the catch that bared her to his warm, hard fingers. She couldn't let this happen, she kept telling herself. It was just a game to him, he didn't mean it. Any minute now he was going to let that seat down and turn her in his arms....

With a wounded cry she pulled out of his arms so suddenly that he was startled into releasing her. She fumbled the door open, deaf to his sharp exclamation, and ran out into the rain.

The long grass beat against her slacks as she ran, not really sure why she was running or where she was trying to go. Seconds later it didn't matter because he'd caught her and dragged her down onto the ground in the wet grass with him.

"Never run from a hunter," he breathed roughly, turning her under him as he found her mouth with his. The rain beat down on them, drenching them, making their bodies as supple as silk-covered saplings, binding them as if there had been no fabric at all in the way.

It was new and exciting to lie like this, to kiss like this, feeling the warm, twisting motions of Ward's big body against hers, their clothes wet and their skin sensitive.

"We might as well have no clothes on at all," he breathed into her open, welcoming mouth, his voice husky with passion. "I can feel you. All of you."

His hands were sliding down her body now, exploring, experiencing her through the wet thinness of fabric, and it was like feeling his hands on her skin.

She moaned as she slid her own hands against his hard-muscled back, his chest, his hips. She didn't understand what was happening, how this passion had crept up on her. But she was lost now, helpless. He could do anything he liked, and she couldn't stop him. She was on fire despite the drenching rain, reaching up toward him, sliding her wet body against his in the silence of the meadow with the rain slicking their hair as it slicked their skin.

He eased his full weight onto her, devouring her mouth with his. His hands smoothed under her back, sensuously pressing her up against him.

Her body throbbed, burned, with the expertness of his movements. Yes, he knew what to do and how to do it. He knew...too much!

"Tell me to stop," he challenged under his breath, probing her lips with his tongue. "Tell me to let you go. I dare you."

"I can't," she whimpered, and her eyes stung with tears as she clung to his broad, wet shoulders. "I want you. Oh, I want you!"

His lips were all over her face. Tender, seeking, gentling, his breath catching in his throat at her devastating submission. He was trembling all over with the force of this new sensation. He wanted to protect her. Devour her. Warm her. Hold her until he died, just like this.

His big hands framed her face as he touched it softly with his lips. "I want to give you a baby," he whispered shakily. "That's what you saw in my face at Wade's, and it made you go red all over. You saw, didn't you?"

"Yes," she whispered back, her body trembling.

He searched her wide eyes, his own blazing with hunger. "I could take you, Marianne," he said very quietly. "Right here. Right now. I could have you, and no one would see us or hear us."

She swallowed, closing her eyes. Defeated. She knew that. She could feel how capable he was of it, and her body trembled under his fierce arousal. She wanted him, too. She loved him more than her honor.

"Yes," she whispered, so softly that he could barely hear.

He didn't move. He seemed to stop breathing. She opened her eyes and saw his face above her, filled with such frank exultation that she blinked incomprehensibly.

"Baby," he breathed softly, bending. He kissed her with such aching tenderness that her eyes stung, tasting her lips, smoothing his lips over her cheeks, her forehead, her nose, her eyes. "Baby, sweet, sweet baby. You taste of roses and gardenias, and I could lie here doing this for all my life."

That didn't sound like uncontrollable passion. It didn't even sound like lust. She reached up and touched his face, his chin.

He kissed the palm of her hand, smiling down at her through wildly exciting shudders. "Do you know how wet you are?" he said with a gentle smile, glancing down at her blouse, which was plastered against breasts that no longer had the shelter of a bra.

"So are you," she replied unsteadily and managed to smile back. What good was pride now when she'd offered herself to him?

He touched her taut nipples through the cloth. "No more embarrassment?" he asked quietly.

"You know what I look like," she whispered.

"Yes." He opened her blouse, no longer interested in the rain that had slowed to a sprinkle, and his eyes feasted on her soft skin before he bent and tasted it warmly with his mouth.

Mari lifted softly toward his lips, savoring their sweet touch, so much a part of him that nothing seemed wrong anymore.

"You're so sweet," he whispered. He drew his cheek across her breasts, his eyes closed, savoring her. "For the rest of my life, I'll never touch another woman like this. I'll never lie with another woman, taste another woman, want another woman."

That was how she felt, too, about other men. She closed her eyes, smoothing his wet hair as he brushed his mouth over her pulsating, trembling body. She loved him so much. If this was all he could give her, it would be enough. Fidelity would do. She couldn't leave him again.

"I'll never want another man," she replied quietly.

He laid his cool cheek against her and sighed, holding her as she held him, with the wind blowing softly and the rain coming down like droplets of silk over them.

Then he moved away, gently rearranging her disheveled clothing. He brushed back her damp hair, kissed her tenderly one last time and carried her in his arms back to the car with her face pressed wetly into his warm throat.

"The car," she faltered. "We'll get the seats wet."

"Hush, baby," he whispered, brushing a kiss against her soft mouth as he put her into the passenger seat and fastened her seat belt. "It doesn't matter. Nothing matters now."

He got in beside her, found her warm hand and linked her fingers with his. He managed to start the car and drive it all the way home with one free hand.

Lillian took one look at them, and her eyebrows shot up.

"Not one word," Ward cautioned as he led Marianne inside. "Not one single word."

Lillian sighed. "Well, at least now you're getting wet together," she murmured with a smile as she wandered back toward the kitchen. "I guess that's better than mildewing alone."

Marianne smiled gently at Ward and went upstairs to change her clothing. He disappeared a few minutes later after an urgent telephone call and drove off by himself with only a wink and a smile for Mari. She walked around in a daze, dodging Lillian's hushed questions, waiting for him to come home. But when bedtime came, he still wasn't back.

Mari went up to her room and paced the floor, worrying, wondering what to do. She couldn't leave, not after this afternoon. He wanted her and she wanted him. Maybe he couldn't offer her marriage, but she'd just settle for what he could give her. He had to care a little. And she loved him enough for both of them.

Why hadn't he gone ahead, she wondered, when he had the chance this afternoon? Why had he stopped? Was he just giving her time to make up her mind, to be sure she could accept him this way? That had to be it. Well, it was now or never.

She put on her one seductive gown, a pretty white one with lots of lace and long elegant sleeves. She brushed out her dark hair until it was smooth and silky and dabbed on perfume. Then, looking in the mirror, she stared into her troubled blue eyes and assured herself that she was doing the right thing.

An hour later she heard Ward drive up. He came up the stairs, pausing at her door. Seconds later he started away, but Mari was already on her feet. She opened the door breathlessly and looked up at him.

He was wearing a dark pair of slacks with a patterned gray shirt open at the throat. His creamy dress Stetson was held in one hand. The other worried his hair. He stared at Mari with eyes that devoured her.

"Dangerous, baby, wearing something like that in front of me," he said softly and smiled.

She swallowed her pride. "I want you," she whispered shakily.

He smiled down at her. "I know. I want you, too."

She opened the door a little wider, her hands unsteady.

He cocked an eyebrow. "Is that an invitation to be seduced?"

She swallowed again. "I don't think I quite know how to seduce you. So I think you'll have to seduce me."

His smile widened. "What about precautions, little temptress?"

She blushed to her toes. She hadn't expected resistance. "Well," she began, peeking up at him, "can't you take care of that?"

His white teeth showed under his lips. "No."

Her blush deepened. "Oh."

He tossed his hat onto the hall table and went inside the room, gently closing the door behind him. "Now, come here." He drew her in front of him, holding her by both shoulders, his face gentle and almost loving. "What do you think I want, Marianne?"

"You've made what you want pretty obvious," she replied sadly.

"What you think I want," he corrected. His eyes went over her like hands, enjoying the exciting glimpses of her silky skin that he was getting through the gossamer-thin fabric of her gown. "And you're right about that. I could make a banquet of you in bed. But not tonight."

She turned her head a bit, looking up at him. "Are you too tired?" she asked innocently.

He grinned. "Nope."

None of this was getting through to her. "I don't understand," she said softly.

"Yes, I gathered that." He reached into his pocket and drew out a box. It was black and velvety and small. He opened it and handed it to her.

The ring was a diamond. A big, beautiful diamond in a setting with lots of little diamonds in rows encircling the large stone. Beside it was a smaller, thinner matching diamond band.

"It's an engagement ring," he explained. "It goes on the third finger of your left hand, and at the wedding I'll put the smaller one on your finger beside it."

She was hearing things. Surely she was! But the ring looked real. She couldn't stop staring at it.

"You don't want to get married," she told him patiently, her eyes big and soft. "You hate ties. You hate women. They're all deceitful and greedy."

He traced a slow, sensuous pattern down her silky cheek, smiling softly. "I want to get married," he said. "I want you to share your life with me."

It was the way he put it. She burst into tears. They rolled down her cheeks in a torrent, a sob broke from her throat. He became a big, handsome blur.

"Now, now," he murmured gently. He bent to kiss the tears away. "It's all right."

"You want to marry me?" she whispered unsteadily.

"Yes," he said, smiling.

"Really?"

"Really." He brushed back her hair, his green eyes possessive on her oval face. "I'd be a fool to let go of a woman who loves me as much as you do."

She froze in place. Was he fishing? Was he guessing? Did he know? If he did, how?

"You told me this afternoon," he said gently, pulling her to him. "You offered yourself to me with no strings. You'd never make an offer like that to a man you didn't love desperately. I knew it. And that's why I stopped. It would have been cheap, somehow, to have our first time on the ground without doing things properly."

"But...but..." she began, trying to find the right words.

"But how do I feel?" he probed softly, touching her lips with a faintly unsteady index finger. "Don't you know?"

His eyes were telling her. His whole face was telling her. But despite her rising excitement, she had to have it all. The words, too.

"Please tell me," she whispered.

He framed her face and lifted it to his darkening eyes, to his firm, hungry mouth. "I love you, Marianne," he breathed against her mouth as he took it. "And this is how much..."

It took him a long time to show her how much. When he was through, they were lying on the bed with her gown down to her waist, and he looked as if he were going to die trying to stop himself from going the whole way. Fortunately, or unfortunately, Lillian had guessed what was going on and was trying to knock the door down.

"It's bedtime, boss," she called loudly. "It's late. She's a growing girl. Needs her sleep!"

"Oh, no, that's not what I need at all," Marianne said with such tender frustration that Ward laughed through his own shuddering need.

"Okay, aunt-to-be," he called back. "Give me a minute to say good-night and I'll be right out."

"You're getting married?" Lillian shouted gleefully.

"That's about the size of it," he answered, smiling down at Mari. "Aren't you just overjoyed with your meddling now?"

"Overjoyed doesn't cover it," Lillian agreed. "Now, speaking as your future aunt-in-law, come out of there! Or wait until supper tomorrow night and see if you get fed! We're going to do this thing right!"

"I was just about to do this thing right," he whispered to Mari, his eyes softly mocking. "Wasn't I?"

"Yes." She laughed. "But we can't admit that."

"We can't?" He sighed. "I guess not."

He got up reluctantly, rebuttoning the shirt that her darting fingers had opened over a chest that was aching for her hands. "Pretty thing," he murmured, watching her pull the gown up again.

"You're pretty, too, so there," she teased.

"Are you coming out, or am I coming in?" Lillian was sounding militant.

Ward glowered at the door. "Can't I even have a minute to say good-night?"

"You've been saying good-night for thirty minutes already, and that's enough," she informed him. "I'm counting! One, two, three..."

She was counting loudly. Ward sighed at Mari. "Good night, baby," he said reluctantly.

She blew him a kiss. "Good night, my darling."

He took one last look and opened the door on "...Fourteen!"

Mari laid back against the pillows, listening to the pleasant murmur of voices outside the door as she stared at her ring.

"Congratulations and good night, dear!" Aunt Lillian called.

"Good night and thank you!" Mari called back.

"Oh, you're very welcome!" Ward piped in.

"Get out of here," Lillian muttered, pushing him down the hall.

Alone in her room Mari was trying to convince herself that she wasn't dreaming. It was the hardest thing she'd ever done. He was hers. They were going to be married. They were going to live together and love each other and have children together. She closed her eyes reluctantly, tingling all over with the first stirrings of possession.

Chapter Twelve

The next morning Mari was sure it had all been a beautiful dream until she looked at the ring on her finger. When she went down to breakfast, she found a new, different Ward waiting for her.

He went to her without hesitation, bending to brush a tender kiss against her smiling lips.

"It was real after all," he murmured, his green eyes approving her cool blue knit sundress. "I thought I might have dreamed it."

"So did I," she confessed. Her hands smoothed hesitantly over the hard, warm muscles of his chest. It felt wonderful to be able to do that, to feel so much a part of him that it no longer was forbidden to touch him, to look at him too long. "Are you really mine now?" she murmured aloud.

"Until I die," he promised, bringing her close against him. He sighed into her hair, rocking her against the powerful muscles of his body. "I never thought this would happen. I didn't think I'd ever be able to love or trust a woman again after Caroline. And then you came along, pushing me into indoor streams, backing me into corners about my business sense, haunting me with your soft innocence. You got under my skin that first night. I've spent the rest of the time trying to convince myself that I was still free when I knew all along that I was hopelessly in love with you."

She burrowed closer, tingling all over at that sweet, possessive note in his deep voice. "I was so miserable in Atlanta," she confessed. "I missed you every single day. I tried to get used to being alone."

"I shouldn't have propositioned you," he said with a sigh, lifting his head to search her eyes with his. "But I still thought I could stop short of a commitment. God knows how I'd have coped with the conscience I didn't even have until you came along. Every time Ty Wade was mentioned, I got my back up, thinking how he'd changed." He touched her face with wonder in his whole look. "And now I know how and why, and I think he must have felt this way with his Erin when he realized what he felt for her."

She sighed softly, loving him with her eyes. "I know I felt like part of me was missing when I left here. It didn't get any better, either."

"Why do you think I came after you?" he murmured dryly. "I couldn't stand it here without you. Not that I admitted that to myself in any great rush. Not until that rattler almost got you, and I had to face it. If anything had happened to you, I wouldn't have wanted to live," he added on a deep, husky note that tugged at her heart.

"I feel that way, too," she whispered, searching his eyes. "Can we really get married?"

"Yes," he whispered back, bending his head down. "And live together and sleep together and raise a family together..."

Her lips opened for him, welcoming and warm, just for a few seconds before Lillian came in with breakfast and knowing grins. Ward glowered at her.

"All your fault," he told her. "I could have gone on for years living like a timber wolf but for you."

"No need to thank me," she said with a big smile. "You're welcome."

She vanished back into the kitchen, laughing, as Ward led Mari to the table, shaking his head with an exasperated chuckle.

The wedding was a week later, and old Mrs. Jessup and Belinda had come home just for the occasion. They sat on either side of Lillian, who was beaming.

"Nice girl," Belinda whispered. "She'll make a new man of him."

"I think she has already." Old Mrs. Jessup grinned. "Spirited little thing. I like her, too."

"I always did," Lillian said smugly. "Good thing I saw the shape he was getting in and brought her out here. I knew they'd be good for each other."

"It isn't nice to gloat," Belinda reminded her.

"Amen," Mrs. Jessup harrumphed. "Don't I seem to remember that you introduced that Caroline creature to him in the first place?"

Lillian was horrified. "That wasn't me! That was Belinda!"

Mrs. Jessup's eyes widened as she glared past Lillian at the restless young woman on the other side. "Did you?"

"It was an accident," Belinda muttered. "I meant to introduce her to Bob Whitman, to get even for jilting me. Ward kind of got in the way. I never meant for her to go after my poor brother."

"It's all in the past now anyway," Lillian said, making peace. "He's got the right girl, now. Everything will be fine."

"Yes." Old Mrs. Jessup sighed, glancing past Lillian again. "If only Belinda would settle down. She goes from boyfriend to boyfriend, but she never seems to get serious."

Lillian pursed her lips, following the older woman's gaze to Belinda, who was sighing over Mari's wedding gown as she walked down the aisle accompanied by the organ music. She'd have to see what she could do....

The wedding ceremony was short and beautiful. Mari thought she'd never seen a man as handsome as her Ward, and when the minister pronounced them husband and wife, she cried softly until Ward kissed away the tears.

Lillian, not Belinda, caught the wedding bouquet and blushed like a schoolgirl when everyone giggled. The guests threw rice and waved them off, and Mari caught a glimpse of tall, slender Ty Wade with his Erin just on the fringe of the guests.

"Alone at last." Ward grinned, glancing at her.

"I thought they'd never leave," she agreed with a wistful sigh. "Where are we going? I didn't even ask."

"Tahiti," he said with a slow smile. "I booked tickets the day after you said yes. We're flying out of San Antonio early tomorrow morning."

"What about tonight?" she asked curiously and flushed at the look on his face.

"Let me worry about tonight," he murmured softly.

He held her hand as he drove, and an hour later he drove up to a huge, expensive hotel in the city.

He'd reserved the bridal suite, and it was the most incredible sight Mari had ever seen. The bed was huge, dominating the bedroom. She stood in the doorway just staring at it while Ward paid the bellhop and locked the door.

"It's huge," she whispered.

"And strategically placed, did you notice?" he murmured with a laugh, suddenly lifting her clear of the floor in her neat white linen traveling suit.

"Yes, I did notice," she said huskily, clinging to him. "You looked so handsome."

"You looked so lovely." He bent to her mouth and started walking. "I love you to distraction, did I tell you?"

"Several times."

"I hope you won't mind hearing it again frequently for the next hour or so," he murmured against her eager mouth and laid her gently down on the bed.

Mari had expected ardor and passion, and she had experienced a tiny measure of apprehension. But he made it so natural, so easy. She relaxed even as he began to undress her, his hands and mouth so deeply imprinted on her memory that she accepted them without the faintest protest.

"This is familiar territory for us, isn't it?" he breathed as he moved back beside her after stripping off his own clothing. "Up to this point, at least," he added at her rapt, faintly shocked visual exploration of him. "But you know how it feels to have my eyes and my hands and my mouth on you. You know that I won't hurt you. That there's nothing to be afraid of."

She looked back up into his eyes. "I couldn't be afraid of you."

"I won't lose control right away," he promised, bending slowly to her mouth. "Give yourself to me now, Mari. Remember how it was on the ground, with the rain soaking us, and give yourself to me the way you offered then."

She felt all over again the pelting rain, the sweetness of his hands, the wild fever of his mouth claiming hers in the silence of the meadow. She reached up to him, suddenly on fire with the unaccustomed removal of all barriers, physical and moral, and she gave herself with an abandon that frankly startled him.

"Shhh," she whispered when he tried to draw back at the last minute, to make it gentle, to keep from hurting her. But she reached up to his hips and softly drew them down again, lifting, and a tiny gasp was the only sound she made as she coaxed his mouth back to hers. "Now," she breathed into his devouring lips. "Now, now..."

"Mari," he groaned. His body surged against hers, his arms became painfully strong, his hands biting into her hips, his mouth trembling as his body trembled. He was part of her. She was part of him. Locking together, loving, linking...

"Mari!"

She went with him on a journey as exquisitely sweet as it was incredibly intimate, yielding to his strength, letting him guide her, letting him teach her. She used muscles she hadn't realized she possessed, she whispered things to him that would shock her later. She wound herself around him and lost all her inhibitions in a wild, fierce joining that ripped the veil of mystery from the sweetest expression of shared love. Even the first time it was still a kind of pleasure that she hadn't known existed.

She stretched lazily, contentedly, and snuggled close to him under the lightweight sheet, nuzzling against his matted chest with a face radiant with fulfillment.

"I love you," he said softly as if the words still awed him. He smoothed her hair tenderly. "I always will."

"I love you just as much." She smoothed her hand over his chest. "Cousin Bud wasn't at the wedding." She frowned. Her mind had been curiously absent for a week. She lifted up. "Ward, Bud hasn't been at the house!"

"Not for a week," he agreed complacently, grinning. "Not since that day I took you to see Ty and Erin."

"But this is horrible! I didn't notice!"

"That's all right, sweetheart, I don't mind," he said, drawing her back down.

"Where is he?"

"Oh, I sent him on a little trip," he murmured at her temple. "I told him that bull he wanted was out to stud at a cattle ranch in Montana, and he went up there looking."

"Looking?" she frowned.

"Well, honey, I didn't exactly tell him which ranch it was on. Just the state. There are a lot of ranches in Montana."

"You devil!" she accused, digging him in the ribs.

He pulled her over him, smiling from ear to ear. "All's fair, don't they say? Cousin Bud always did cramp my style." He coaxed her mouth down to his and kissed it softly. "I didn't want him on my case until I had you safely married to me."

"You couldn't have been jealous?"

"I've always been jealous," he confessed, tugging a strand of her hair playfully. "You were mine. I didn't want him trying to cut me out. Don't worry, he'll figure it out eventually."

"I shouldn't ask," she mumbled. "Figure what out?"

"That the bull is still on my ranch, just where I had him all along."

"What are you going to tell Cousin Bud?"

"That I misplaced him," he said easily. "Don't worry, he'll believe me. After all, he didn't think I was serious about you, either, and look how I fooled him!"

She would have said something else, but he was already rolling her over on the big bed and kissing the breath out of her. So she just closed her eyes and kissed him back. Outside it was raining softly, and Mari thought she'd never heard a sweeter sound.

Silhouette Romance

COMING NEXT MONTH

FAMILY AFFAIR—Rita Rainville
Brady wanted to marry the right woman—Sara Clayton. And
with the help of five elderly friends and one orangutan, he set out
to win her love.

GIFT OF THE GODS—Judith McWilliams
Rescuing her teenage "charge" from the hands of wealthy Greek
Philip Stephanos turned out to be easier than rescuing herself—
especially when Sophie discovered she didn't want to be rescued!

A MAN FOR SYLVIA—Sue Santore
What was the mystery of the velvet painting? Could it be behind
the accidents befalling Sylvia? With Craig's help, Sylvia probed
the puzzling secrets of the picture—and her heart.

THE FOREVER KIND—Karen Young
When Jill's little boy disappeared, it was old friend
Sam Halloran to the rescue. But finding Josh was easier than
convincing Jill to take another chance on love—and Sam.

FOR EACH TOMORROW—Curtiss Ann Matlock
It had been years since Quent left town. Now he was back—a
dashing Oklahoma Ranger—and after Cassie's heart. Cassie
didn't want to give it to him. But she soon learned that in order to
gain, you had to risk—and that the reward was worth the price.

NO QUESTIONS ASKED—Lynnette Morland
Conn Tomelty, celebrated journalist, was doing a story on
Lifeline, a disaster relief organization. But what he really wanted
to research was its newly appointed director, Rosalie Madden.

AVAILABLE THIS MONTH

UNLIKELY LOVER
Diana Palmer

THE CASTAWAYS
Frances Lloyd

FRIENDS—AND THEN SOME
Debbie Macomber

HEAVENLY MATCH
Sharon De Vita

THE EYES OF A STRANGER
Terri McGraw

HERO ON HOLD
Glenda Sands

ATTRACTIVE, SPACE SAVING BOOK RACK

Display your most prized novels on this handsome and sturdy book rack. The hand-rubbed walnut finish will blend into your library decor with quiet elegance, providing a practical organizer for your favorite hard-or soft-covered books.

Only $9.95

Approximately 16" x 8" when assembled

Assembles in seconds!

To order, rush your name, address and zip code, along with a check or money order for $10.70 ($9.95 plus 75¢ postage and handling) (New York residents add appropriate sales tax),payable to *Silhouette Reader Service* to:

In the U.S.

Silhouette Reader Service
Book Rack Offer
901 Fuhrmann Blvd.
P.O. Box 1325
Buffalo, NY 14269-1325

Offer not available in Canada.

BKR-2

Silhouette Desire

**Available
January 1987**

NEVADA
SILVER

The third book in the exciting
Desire Trilogy by Joan Hohl.

The Sharp brothers are back, along with
sister Kit...and Logan McKittrick.

Kit's loved Logan all her life and, with a little
help from the silver glow of a Nevada night,
she must convince the stubborn rancher that
she's a woman who needs a man's love—not
the protection of another brother.

Don't miss *Nevada Silver*—Kit and
Logan's story and the conclusion
of Joan Hohl's acclaimed
Desire Trilogy.